Cravings

Cravings

Cravings

GARNETT KILBERG COHEN

THE UNIVERSITY OF WISCONSIN PRESS

The University of Wisconsin Press
728 State Street, Suite 443
Madison, Wisconsin 53706
uwpress.wisc.edu

Gray's Inn House, 127 Clerkenwell Road
London EC1R 5DB, United Kingdom
eurospanbookstore.com

Printed in the United States of America
This book may be available in a digital edition.

Library of Congress Cataloging-in-Publication Data

Names: Cohen, Garnett Kilberg, author.
Title: Cravings / Garnett Kilberg Cohen.
Description: Madison, Wisconsin : The University of Wisconsin Press, 2023.
Identifiers: LCCN 2023005962 | ISBN 9780299345242 (paperback)
Subjects: LCGFT: Short stories.
Classification: LCC PS3553.O4228 C73 2023 | DDC 813/.54—dc23/eng/20230620
LC record available at https://lccn.loc.gov/2023005962

This is a work of fiction. The stories are products of the author's imagination.
Although actual places and events inspired parts of some stories, the incidents
are used fictitiously. Any character resemblance to actual persons living or dead
is unintended.

The true history of life is but a history of moments.
It is only at rare moments we live.
—SHERWOOD ANDERSON

Contents

Cravings

Hors d'oeuvres

I. Childhood (1980s)

Whenever Cassie's parents had a cocktail party or hosted bridge night, Cassie waited until no one was around and hoisted herself up onto the kitchen counter. Her thin arms wobbled until her knees—one knee, then the other—felt firmly planted. She took a few breaths before she stood on her feet and found her balance. Tilting slightly backward, she tiptoed along the linoleum ledge, searching the top cupboards for hidden treats: peanuts, fancy crackers, and tall jars of olives. Her parents knew her appetite for such things was unquenchable, yet rather than strictly forbid her from attacking the party food, they hid it.

The smallness of the food—meals for birds or dolls—excited her. Spread out on trays, the snacks looked like an exotic miniature feast. Cheese puffs, crackers with waves of cream cheese, pizzas the size of silver dollars, and tiny hot dogs wrapped in Pillsbury dough so that they made her think of pink babies in white swaddling blankets. Any one of these savories was more appealing than having to eat through the large sameness of a turkey breast or a pork chop. At meals, her parents often had to goad her to eat. It was the salty taste she really craved, the zing that flashed through her system on the first contact with the tip of her tongue, the way the tang made her upper body quake and shiver.

So when her father hauled the card tables up from the basement on a snowy Saturday a week before her eighth birthday, Cassie's salivary glands ached at the sight of them. Somewhere in the far reaches of the cupboards lurked crackers and olives. Her mother had taken her older brother, Todd, to a Cub Scout meeting at the other den mother's house, so the kitchen was clear of her for the entire afternoon. Cassie only needed to get rid of her father. Usually she wanted time alone with him, time when he might notice her. He was a good father to Todd, coached his little league team and helped him earn scout merit badges. Todd had more than twenty embroidered insignias sewn to his sash. Next year, Todd was primed to leave the cubs for Boy Scouts, and Cassie's father was going to be a troop leader.

He and Todd spent hours poring over maps, searching for camping and hiking spots. Cassie's father was also a doting husband. He adored Cassie's mother. They still held hands. Yet he didn't seem to know what to do with Cassie. Occasionally he played board games with her, but his mind usually seemed elsewhere. She had to remind him when his turn arrived. If not for the card tables, she would have tried to coax him into a game that afternoon. Instead, she wanted to be rid of him.

He worked on charts and yellow legal pads at the mahogany dining-room table, making frequent trips into the kitchen to refresh his Diet Coke. There, he stood by the sink, leaning against the edge, absentmind-edly sipping and staring out the window at the swirling snow. Lean and athletic, he had inch-long ginger hair that he mussed into what looked like a scruffy patch of dry lawn while he concentrated on his papers or built things with Todd. When he left for the office on weekday mornings, his tie swinging back and forth against his lean torso, he combed his hair back.

Cassie sat on a chair at the kitchen table, sweeping the tip of her big toe inside her right white sock in arches against the floor, watching it slowly collect dust, waiting for an opportunity. After the fourth or fifth trip, when her father had a full glass, it almost seemed safe to embark on her quest. How much could he drink? But, just as she edged off her chair, she heard the sudden sound of crumpled paper and he stomped into the kitchen to toss a wad in the trash. No, he was too close to take a risk.

At least since he didn't notice Cassie much, he didn't try to force her into a constructive activity. If her mother had been home she would have insisted Cassie tug on her bothersome rubber boots that always became twisted and stuck and go outside for exercise. Build a snowperson or slide down the tiny slope of their backyard in her red plastic snow saucer. Her father would never think of such a thing. Yet, as withdrawn as he could be, he would be worse than her mother if he found her walking along the counter or hiding in a corner gorging on olives. Normally a reasonable man, his anger could flare quickly. In such moments, a vein jutted across his brow like a flash of lightning. Once he had spanked her so hard that he had left a pink imprint of his hand on her bare behind, almost as deep as the white plaster cast of her hands that she had made in first grade. The image of his large, pink fingers had fascinated her. She was sorry when it faded. But she certainly did not want to feel the sting of such a slap ever again.

"Do you want a bologna sandwich or a banana or something?" he asked. No, she shook her head. The thought of chewing her way through either made her sick. She wanted olives or pretzels.

Cassie sat at the kitchen table, looked down at her favorite pink-cotton turtleneck. As her father sipped yet another Coke, Cassie slumped forward and smoothed the fabric of her shirt, thinking that her flat belly curving inward would form a capital C. She was ready to give up. She didn't think he *could* go anywhere. She was too young to be left alone, so it felt like a miracle occurred when he said—more to his Diet Coke than to her—"It's really piling up out there. Your mother will be home soon. I better shovel the drive."

Cassie's throat ached in anticipation as she watched him slip his arms into the sleeves of his down coat and wrap his Burberry scarf around his neck. Once he was outside, she watched him through the hallway window as he went to the garage for the shovel. As soon as he sank the blade into the snow at the foot of the drive, Cassie ran back to the kitchen, pulled off her socks for better traction, and heaved herself up onto the counter. She arched her back, drew her chin in, and walked along, pulling open cupboard doors and sticking her balsa-wood-thin right arm into the far, dark reaches of the upper cupboard. She grabbed at the empty space.

Cupboard one.

Cupboard two.

Cupboard three.

Ah, a smooth glass cylinder, shoved too far back to grasp. She wiggled her fingers. Two containers! Slowly, she rolled the nearest one forward with her fingertips until she had worked the jar halfway across the cupboard. She felt a cramp in her leg and her neck was stiff. She kept working, her jaw and the root of her tongue throbbing at the thought of the olive juice, until her palm was firmly wrapped around the glass. When she had it, Cassie turned slowly around and sank to her haunches, then sat on the counter edge so that her legs, clad in white-and-pink checked corduroy pants, dangled over the side. She put her whole weight into twisting off the top.

The first olive was the best. An absolute explosion in her mouth!

Her plan had been to eat only the top layer—four to six olives—so that the jar would look untouched. Her parents might notice that it didn't make a popping sound when they opened the lid, but since there would be no rancid smell, they would probably serve them anyway. And even if they threw them away, it wouldn't hurt Cassie. In fact, she could pick them out of the trash later, rinse off the coffee grinds and egg yolks. Thinking about finding lone olives in the trash—green-and-red jewels—reignited her appetite. She ate beyond the first six, then beyond the first ten. After that, each successive olive was a little less satisfying, but she kept going. The jar was half-empty before she stopped. She slipped off the counter and went to peer out the hall window. Her father had shoveled less than half of the driveway. She returned to the olives.

"Why not?" she asked aloud to herself. That was what her mother always said before she did something adventurous. Besides, Cassie might have a better chance of going undetected if the jar was gone. They still had a full jar left for their party—they might even think they had only purchased one. She lined the remaining olives along the counter like a conveyer belt and walked down, sucking each one into her mouth. Such a luxury! Afterward, she drank the brine that remained in the jar. The liquid salt made her feel a little queasy, but she knew she would never have such an opportunity again. She buried the empty jar and lid at the bottom of the trash. When a ring pierced the silence, she jumped back as if she had been caught. Cassie laughed when she realized it was only the phone. Her laugh reminded her a little of the cackle of the depraved, wicked witch in Oz.

It was her mother.

"Cassie, put your father on."

"He's outside shoveling."

"Urrrgh," her mother growled. "My damn car is stuck in the Kellys' driveway. And I've got to get ready for the party. Could you two get over here so he can help Dick Kelly get it out?"

"I'll go tell him," Cassie said and hung up the phone.

She opened the front door without bothering to put on her socks. The swirling snow and wind that blew into the front hall felt strange against her body without proper gear to protect her. She had to call out to her father three times before he looked up and saw her. He shoved up the blue knit cap, uncovering his ears.

"Mom needs you at the Kellys' house. Her car is stuck," Cassie shouted against the wind.

Her father's shoulders slumped. The snow piled in his shovel was as white and high as the cake at her aunt's wedding. The section he had cleared had already accumulated another fresh half inch. He tossed the shovel in the yard and shook his head. The wedding cake heap fell to the side, like a hollow mound of sugar.

"Go get . . ." he started to say, and then seemed to think better of it—did he want to avoid the work it would be getting her into her boots, coat, hat, scarf, and mittens? Or avoid the intimacy of it? "Do you think you could stay here by yourself for just a little while? The Kellys are just a ten-minute drive."

"Sure," Cassie shouted. Her mind raced to the second jar of olives. No, no, she had to find the pretzels. Her hair and pink turtleneck were getting wet from the snow.

"Close the door," he said. "You're letting all the heat out."

She had the entire house to herself. Such a luxury! But her stomach roiled, and for the first time, she wasn't sure her system could handle more salt. She found an antidote in the refrigerator, hidden behind the milk and the baking powder: a small jar of neon-red maraschino cherries. She didn't crave sugar as much as salt, but when she did have something sweet she preferred the unnaturally charged sweetness of the most saccharine of sugary candy to the natural sweetness of fresh fruit, so the cherries were perfect. The jar was even open. She carried it into the family room to eat leisurely in front of the television. Cassie ate slowly as she watched a rerun of *The Addams Family*. She liked Wednesday Addams's coyness, her big eyes, and her dark dresses. Cassie wondered what her parents would think if she took to wearing dresses all of the time. Cassie treated each cherry like a tiny apple, using just one front upper tooth and one front lower tooth to take tiny bites. She was proud that it took her the entire show to eat just three cherries. While the credits rolled, Cassie took one small lady-like sip of the glowing-red cherry juice, resealed the top, and went in search of pretzels. The hunt was almost too easy. In the broom closet, the second place she looked, Cassie found an enormous family-sized bag on the floor behind the mop and bucket. She used a fork to tear a small slit in the back of the bag to wiggle pretzels free. Most of the bag remained intact. Her parents probably wouldn't notice the slit, and if they did, her mother would just say, "That damn store," and think nothing more of it.

After she had eaten three pretzels, Cassie noticed the room had grown dark. Her stomach felt settled. She switched on the overhead light and looked longingly up at the cupboard that held the second jar of olives. She thought of how wonderful a pretzel would taste with an olive wedged in each of the holes made by the twists.

She debated. Her parents should have been home already. At any second, she would hear first her mother's car and then her father's turning into the drive, their headlights casting curving lights against the kitchen wall. The thought of the headlights convinced her. They would provide enough warning for her to actually drag a chair to the counter and create a stairway. As soon as the lights appeared, she could quickly reseal the lid and climb down. There wasn't any danger of consuming the entire jar, given how little time she had. She would only eat one olive-festooned pretzel.

Holding just one pretzel (to guard against overindulging), she climbed up onto the chair, and from the chair onto the counter. She leaned back, holding tentatively to the support bar between the cupboards as not to squish her pretzel, and reached into the dark interior. It took longer to get this jar than the first one, partly because it was farther back and partly because the nausea had returned. When she finally had the glass column, she turned around, unwound the lid, and tucked the tilted jar into the smooth fabric of her armpit, pressing as hard as she could to keep the jar pinned to her side. She held the pretzel with the hand of the arm pinned to her side and used her free hand to remove a few olives to decorate the pretzel. As she pulled out the first olive, juice splashed on her arm. She knew it was a risky operation, dependent on luck and balance.

The reflections of car headlights raced across the wall. Cassie jerked around and the tall jar slid

from under her arm,

hit the edge of the counter,

spewed juice,

then crashed

onto the floor

in an oily heap of olives, surrounded by glass petal shards.

Cassie couldn't believe her bad luck. She shoved the entire pretzel in her mouth, bowing out her cheeks like airplane wings, and chewed as she climbed down. She stuck the bag of pretzels in the broom closet, grabbed the broom, and tried to sweep the mess. If she got it under the table, maybe they wouldn't notice until she had time to clean it up, maybe while her mother was dressing for their party. But the broom bristles just brushed over the olives, spreading the juice and sending a few shards of broken glass skittering.

The doorbell rang.

Cassie grasped the broom lower, her hands just above the brush, and batted more ferociously at the clump of olives. A half dozen on the top rolled free, scattering in different directions like baby pool balls.

The doorbell rang again. It was no use; they would be even more upset if they had to stand outside in the blizzard. Cassie leaned the broom against the wall by the table and headed for the door.

Why were they even ringing the bell?

She opened the front door and was surprised to see Mrs. Kelly, her golden-colored hair iced with a thick layer of snow, standing on the porch. Cassie felt a surge of relief.

"There's been an accident," said Mrs. Kelly.

Her relief was replaced with confusion. Cassie stood, uncomprehending.

"Your father has been in an accident. Your mother and brother are at the hospital. Please let me inside."

Cassie stood back.

"What happened?" she asked.

"His car slid off the road. Don't worry," said Mrs. Kelly, unpeeling her coat and dropping it on an armchair just inside the living room as she passed Cassie. She smoothed Cassie's hair, an unusually affectionate and intimate gesture for Mrs. Kelly. "Everything is going to be fine. Just watch some television. I'm going to make a few phone calls for your mother."

Mrs. Kelly headed for kitchen. Cassie hung up Mrs. Kelly's coat. It was heavy and wet and Cassie had a hard time maneuvering it and keeping the sleeves on the flimsy wire hanger, but she knew how much her father hated to see coats flung about. Cassie was surprised that there wasn't a shriek from Mrs. Kelly at the sight of the olives. She waited a few minutes before going into the kitchen to face Mrs. Kelly's reaction. But when she got there, Mrs. Kelly was calmly sweeping the olives into a dustpan, the phone tucked under her chin.

"A car lost control, ice under the snow. Lou slid to avoid it. No. Yes. Yes. No. St. Thomas Memorial—it was the closest. No, I'm here with their daughter."

Intent on her conversation, Mrs. Kelly didn't even glance up at Cassie or ask what had happened with the olives. Cassie's stomach was roiling again. She headed for the television room as instructed. The doorbell rang again. They were home already! Cassie imagined her father's arm in a sling. She ran for the door.

This time it was Trish and Ed Gordon on the porch. Mr. Gordon stood behind his wife, who was wearing a red wool coat that matched her deep-red lipstick. The red stood out against the snow almost like cutout images. She held a round bowl covered in aluminum foil and looked down into Cassie's face. The Gordons were closer friends of her parents than they were of Mrs. Kelly's.

"We're a little early," said Mrs. Gordon. "Are your parents still getting ready?"

Cassie didn't think she should say the word "accident" aloud; it would make it sound worse than it was. The Gordons looked at her curiously. She heard Mrs. Kelly hang up the phone and rush out behind her.

Trish laughed.

"You're here? I thought you said bridge was a game for our parents' generation." She handed Mrs. Kelly the plate and said, "Some shrimp left over from Ed's office party. With the roads so bad, we didn't want to bother going home first, came straight from the office. Everyone was heading out, no need for the hors d'oeuvres to go to waste."

Cassie thought she said "all those ordered to go to waste." It didn't make sense.

Mrs. Kelly placed the bowl on the small table beside the door and, to the astonishment of the Gordons, stepped out onto the porch in the swirling snow with them, pulling the door partially shut behind her. Cassie could just hear the first few sentences of what Mrs. Kelly said before her words were carried away by the howl of the snowy night.

"There's been an accident. I'm calling people for Barb, to cancel. Her address book is here and, well, there was no point taking Cassie out in this storm." She lowered her voice. Cassie only caught a few words. "It doesn't look good . . ."

Cassie peeled back a corner of the foil gripping the bowl. It was filled with fat curls of white shrimp floating in red sauce. She knew they were shrimp, but with Mrs. Gordon's words still echoing in her brain, Cassie couldn't connect the fleshy white pieces with the fancy party food she usually loved.

II. Adulthood (the Rest of Her Life)

For Cassie, adulthood began shortly before her eighth birthday, immediately following her father's funeral. The first six months, the house was quiet. Her mother spent a lot of time napping. She never mentioned the olives. Her brother was rarely home. Their grandmother stayed with them on and off. Of course Cassie felt guilty, as if her ferocious appetite, her hunger and greed, had somehow contributed to her father's death.

Less than a year after her father died, Cassie's mother returned to work as a data analyst.

"Just a few years earlier than we planned," she told Trish Gordon as they sat at the kitchen table. Cassie's mother had taken up smoking again. She rolled the growing tip of her ash against the side of the homemade ashtray Cassie had molded for Mother's Day in first grade, the same year that Cassie had made the cast of her hands that resembled the imprint of her father's spanking. A big year for crafts. Perhaps the last year that any child made an ashtray gift in a public school. Cassie stood outside their line of vision. Over the next few years, she would find herself standing just out of sight quite often, eavesdropping, trying to figure out what she had missed. This time, she could only see their hands, two right fingers of Mrs. Gordon's right hand looping the handle of her coffee mug, the thumb on top of the handle for balance. She lifted the mug out of Cassie's eyesight. "He was underinsured. Just the company policy. After all, he was in perfect health."

The next year, they sold the house and moved into a rented duplex just outside of town. Todd did not go on to Boy Scouts as he had planned. Instead he took up skateboarding and smoking pot. Their mother was always harried and didn't have much time for them, certainly no time to be a troop leader, if they even took women at that time. And Cassie imagined that Todd didn't want to think about Scouts any more than she wanted to think of gorging herself on olives and maraschino cherries. There weren't many bananas in the house anymore, mostly junk food, seldom olives and never maraschino cherries. When there were olives, Cassie still craved them but never allowed herself to eat more than one a day.

Her mother didn't tell them when she started dating, so it was a bit of a surprise when, shortly before Cassie's twelfth birthday, she announced she was getting married to Tom Wilson, whom Cassie had only met twice. After that, there were a few awkward dinners and outings to the movies and the skating rink. "Tom," as she was told to call him, looked nothing like her father. While her father had seemed hard and sleek, Tom was soft and pudgy, with curly hair and a double chin.

"Why not?" Cassie's mother said on the phone to a woman friend and laughed.

Cassie asked her if she was going to wear a white gown and have a big reception like her Aunt Linda had had when Cassie was six. "No, no," said Cassie's mother with a laugh. Her frequent napping and overall harried behavior had been replaced with unexpected bursts of laughter and gaiety. "We're going to get married in a judge's chambers, just the two of us, you and Todd, Tom's son Michael, and the Gordons as witnesses. Then we'll have people over for champagne and hors d'oeuvres at Tom's house."

Cassie's brain seized at the term. Even though she knew her mother had not said *ordered*, she understood immediately that it was the same strange expression that Mrs. Gordon had used. The way her mother said it, the words sounded more like *or-serves*. But Cassie knew that wasn't it either.

"What are *or-serves*?" asked Cassie. She blurred the words and said them quickly so that her mother wouldn't know she couldn't pronounce them.

"*Hors d'oeuvres*," her mother corrected anyway, though Cassie didn't notice a big difference in the sound of how she said it with the way her mother did. "It's a type of food."

"How do you spell that?" asked Cassie.

Her mother spelled it twice. Cassie had to write it down. She had only recently learned the word *whore*, though not how to spell it, and she wondered if the two words had a connection. How could a whore be connected to food? Before her mother left the room, she added, "oh, we're going to be moving into Tom's house. You're going to love it! You'll have a huge bedroom."

There was a whole chapter in her mother's *Joy of Cooking* on hors d'oeuvres as "appetizers served with drinks" and named canapés, cheese balls, and olives as possibilities. In another cookbook, she looked up *appetizer*, though he felt she knew what it meant. To her amazement, the description read "excites a desire for more." For a minute—only a minute—she felt a little relief. The accident didn't seem entirely her fault.

Cassie's mother and Tom got married in a judge's paneled chambers. On one of the judge's walls hung an enormous bulletin board with photos of all the couples he had married. Cassie wore a peach-colored corsage, a smaller version of her mother's. Todd rolled his eyes and twisted his lips and looked angry, which had become his general mood. Despite the fact that Cassie now knew the correct definition for hors d'oeuvres and that she believed that her mother had every right to remarry, Cassie's mind went in a loop during the ceremony, thinking over and over, "that whore's got nerve, that whore's got nerve." Afterward, the judge snapped a photo of Cassie's mother and Tom Wilson. The five members of the new family, the judge, and the Gordons all stood around the camera and watched as the image of the new Mr. and Mrs. Tom Wilson rolled—curling and slick—out of the camera and was thumbtacked to the bulletin board.

Tom Wilson's house was bigger than the house Cassie's parents had owned. When they arrived after the ceremony, the kitchen was busy with caterers making trays of hors d'oeuvres. Cassie was shown her new bedroom, where she would move after her mother returned from her honeymoon. Cassie and Todd would stay with their grandmother until then. Cassie's new room was nicer than either of her previous rooms, but it didn't seem real. Everything matched. Her mother had decorated the entire room in pink to surprise her. Cassie had stopped liking pink a long time ago.

When the guests started arriving, Cassie sat in a corner of the kitchen, watching the two cooks slide trays in and out of the oven. Her mouth went crazy—her salivary glands howling, pings of little arrows shooting off the roof of her mouth, miniscule bubbles bursting—at the sight of the pastry puffs, tiny crab cakes, cheesy spinach pies, sausages, and, of course, the olives. An institutional-sized jar sat on the counter wedged between the flapping door to the dining room and the door that led into the attached garage. The curved glass magnified the green meat of the orbs. The cooks used the olives for appetizers and every twenty minutes or so the bartender came in and scooped out a bowl. Cassie bided her time. The first moment she was alone in the kitchen, she shot for the counter, slid the jar off and hugged it to her belly, and slyly slid out the door into the garage where two metallic trash cans stood. She lifted the lid of the one nearest the door, found it only half full. She lowered the sloshing jar down into the bottom of the can, digging it beneath the trash, and then piled the garbage from the other trash can on top. She exited the garage to the outside, reentered the house by the front door, and took her place in the corner of a couch by the fireplace.

Years in the pink room went by quickly. Todd and her stepfather didn't get along, and he went away to live with their grandparents and, later, for the rest of his life, was in and out of rehab. Through middle school and the beginning of high school, Todd's endless fights with their stepfather seemed unbearably long. Later they became barely a blip in her memory. After Cassie turned fifteen, she and her older stepbrother started an on-and-off surreptitious romance, having long make-out sessions all over the house when their parents weren't home, even though he had an "official" girlfriend his own age outside the house. He was angelically handsome, with soft curls and skin as pale and smooth as beeswax. Though he was not pudgy like his father, Cassie could see that like his father, he would turn to fat when he grew older. When she was sixteen and he was nineteen, home on college break, he deflowered her in the pink bedroom. Afterward, while she reclined in his arms, she asked him what his mother's last words had been. She had died after what Cassie's stepfather called a "long battle with cancer" (Cassie always imagined her in full armor, warding off gigantic cells with a slashing sword). He said he didn't know his mother's last words. Cassie wondered if that was better than being stuck with the banality of her father's final words to her:

Close the door. You're letting all the heat out.

Life seemed—alternately, paradoxically, simultaneously, and inexplicably—totally meaningless and so ripe with significance that every word, image, and gesture were connected to another moment in her life. Cassie was a bridesmaid when her stepbrother married his "official" high school sweetheart. The bridesmaids wore dresses the same pink color of her bedroom. The Christmas after college graduation, Cassie wondered if her brother noted the irony of a troop of Boy Scouts singing carols when she visited him at the rehabilitation center. In Mexico, when she was just beginning as an archeologist, instead of feeling echoes of ancient wonder as she climbed her first Mayan pyramid, she flashed back to climbing from the kitchen chair onto the counter in a quest for olives. She never applied lipstick without thinking of Trish Gordon's red mouth and red coat and imagining what her father's red blood must have looked like against the white snow. But what amazed her most was how no one would have ever guessed the way the scenes of her life sped through her brain at any event or cocktail party where she used a toothpick to spear the one olive, round and green and red, she allowed herself on such an evening.

Slow Dance

Dance me to the end of love.
—LEONARD COHEN

We thought we were old when we met. I was thirty-nine and he was forty-three—ages that seem young now. I was divorced and Sam was still single. A few friends said that was a red flag, a guy who had never married. But it wasn't *never* yet, and he had lived with two women, and we would marry later. We went through the standard exchange of life stories and what I now suspect were dates he carefully planned for variety and originality— performance art in Chicago storefronts, a Japanese dance festival, out-of-the-way art exhibits. I had no way of knowing what sorts of dates were typical. My children were both in college: Mia in her first year at Wesleyan and Jacob a junior at University of Illinois. I was on my own for the first time in twenty years. Sam was the third man I had dated in the year since the divorce. I felt I had behaved badly with the first two, so I was determined to do better.

Harvey, the first man I dated, was a friend of a friend. He was nearly fifty, which seemed ancient at the time, and a widower. He had a beard that smelled of flavored pipe smoke, which made me not want to kiss him, yet I did. That was my first bad act, kissing a person I didn't want to kiss. We even made out once, my lips swimming in the fur of his cherry-smelling beard. He was wealthy and witty, had lost his wife to cancer, and took me to expensive restaurants. I would have delivered the line about "just being friends" sooner than I did, except I liked telling people I was dating and no one else had asked me yet. The first time he started to unbutton my blouse, I said, "No, I'm not ready." That was a lie, implying that I would be ready in the future. His next attempt, I felt a little nauseated from the pipe aroma, so I simply, wordlessly, pushed him away—my palm shoving his chest. He exploded (mildly; he was a mild man), saying, "What's the big deal? ! Are your tits made of gold?"

I pictured the girl from *Goldfinger*. My older foster brother took me to see the movie when I was seven. At the time, pre-cable, it was considered racy, not appropriate for a child. My foster brother rarely took me places alone as a child. I don't know what prompted that excursion, probably trying to fill time alone with me when he was stuck babysitting, not realizing that it was a movie that our foster mother would find improper. I remember sensing his arms stiffening beside me when the camera scanned the long bikinied body of the golden girl.

Since Harvey's remark, I have pictured my breasts as golden at the most inopportune times, a gleaming gold lamé, like the girl in *Goldfinger*, only in my imagination, my breasts are stiff and solid, metallic, not malleable like the girl's in the movie.

I met the second man I dated at a Halloween party that was held in a rambling old house of fading elegance in the Prairie Avenue District, an island of mansions just south of the Loop that had reached its peak shortly after the Great Chicago Fire. It had been on the decline, albeit with a few upticks, ever since. The aging hosts were considered part of Chicago's intellectual elite, radical in their day. Their party had been going on for decades and had achieved legendary stature, both for its fame-tinged guests (artists, actors, reporters, advertising folks, and local celebrities) and the inventiveness of the costumes. A man wearing armor made completely of bottle caps clinked from room to room. A Vincent Van Gogh with a bloody patch on the side of his head and an ear dangling around his neck set up an easel in the crowded kitchen and sketched wickedly accurate caricatures of other guests. A woman (supposedly a big shot at Leo Burnett) wore a flawless reproduction of a Heinz ketchup bottle, her face between the bottle and white cap, stained a scary red, framed by a long, red wig. I had never been to the exclusive party before and was invited rather last minute, along with a group of friends at another party, so my costume was an odd mix of what I owned that seemed glittery and costume-like, though not actually representative of anything. My friends and I became separated early on. I stood in front of myriad appetizers spread out on a field-sized dining room table, staring at a platter of hardboiled eggs decorated with olive slices to resemble eyeballs, when Rocky approached me. He was dressed as a Minotaur, wearing a shaggy wig sprouting curly horns, a ring in his nose, and a T-shirt and hairy vest above light-brown tights with a swirly tail attached right above his bottom's crack. The muscles in his butt were so well-defined by the thin tights that his behind—along with his twitching tail—almost seemed obscene.

"I'll eat one if you do," he said. We both laughed—tittered really—but didn't eat any of the eggs. Instead, we started talking, then wandered into a living room or parlor—his forearm and my upper arm brushing—and danced with a half dozen others to oldies like the "Monster Mash," twisting lower and lower until our churning knees were only inches from the tattered Oriental carpet. We did ironic imitations of the Swim and the Jerk until we became breathless, and our laughter turned genuine. Later, we talked art and politics and our jobs as we drifted from room to room. He was a food photographer and I was in public relations, so there was a bit of crossover in our careers and acquaintances, at least with the food companies I represented. We drifted to the wide front porch. On the top step, he pushed his tail away and we sat side by side. It was a warm night and a lot of people were outside. Harmonica music and the smell of pot wafted about. But we were in our own bubble.

A couple dressed as mimes in striped shirts with powder-white faces—the man carrying a sleeping toddler—skirted around us.

"Night, Rocky," said the woman. "Can't believe it's almost one. We've got to get this one home."

Rocky saluted them, then whispered to me under his breath, "Lucky for us we don't have kids."

That's when I should have said, "I do," and told him about Mia and Jacob away at college. I was both surprised at not having mentioned them in all our hours of conversation and enjoying feeling unencumbered, so I didn't. Why couldn't I be fancy-free for a night? When the sky turned pink and he asked me for my phone number, it seemed crazy to say, "And oh, by the way, I actually do have two children who are almost adults."

We went on three dates. Each time, I felt guiltier, as if I had killed Mia and Jacob or orphaned them. I preferred the orphan scenario; at least as orphans they had each other and I had been punished for my sin of omission. By our second date, I had stopped being able to concentrate on our conversations, focusing, instead, on trying to find a way to casually break the news of my offspring. Rocky lived in the Pilsen neighborhood and I lived on the north side. Chicago is a big city, but not that big. And our professions did overlap. I didn't want him to find out on his own.

On our last date, sitting across from each other at a Thai restaurant, he told me that I looked like a young Katharine Ross, a generous comparison I thought. He was extremely handsome, with a large head and lustrous black curls. He almost could have been a Minotaur without a costume. His mother was of Mexican descent and his father, Italian. The only actors I could think of to compare him to seemed like stereotypes of his heritage, so I remained silent.

We exchanged ages. He was thirty-two.

"You look too young to be thirty-nine!" he said with a big smile. "Show me your license!"

I showed him.

"No one would guess from looking at you," he said.

I thought of saying "or that I have two grown kids." Instead I talked about my trip to the Grand Canyon the summer before as if I had traveled there by myself.

"I'm glad you're older and you didn't lie about your age. For once, I'm with a woman who doesn't play head games," he said. "After my last relationship, I've been pretty starved for maturity and honesty."

If that wasn't a perfect opportunity, there never would be one. So I told him about my children.

~

I met Sam six weeks later. After what happened with Rocky, I knew to tell Sam about my kids within the first ten minutes of our introduction.

"How old?" he asked.

"They're both in college,"

"That's a relief! I was scared you were going to say they're little kids. I'm not into kids."

I found his remark a bit presumptive and arrogant, but I was so relieved that I hadn't killed off my children again that I let it go.

Sam was a dentist (still is, though retirement looms), a profession that had previously seemed nerdy to me if I thought about it at all. Or worse, the occupation of a person who couldn't get into medical school, so had to settle. With Sam, I began to see things differently. The way he described dentistry made it sound artistic—matching colors and sizes of little gems, working in tiny spaces. He talked of teeth the way his great-grandparents probably discussed diamonds when they were in Antwerp, and later his grandparents in the States. Sam's father had broken the tradition and become a physician, and it turned out that Sam *had* gone to med school, though chose to drop out in his third year.

"I shadowed two docs in my father's practice and just didn't find it that interesting, so little variety. Just writing prescriptions and looking down people's throats or up their asses," he said. "I asked my dentist if I could shadow him for a day. He agreed and it was fascinating—so many different problems to solve. My parents weren't too happy about my decision since my dad planned to pass on his practice, but they wanted me to be happy, and they understood—it wasn't like my dad wanted to be a diamond broker and take over his dad's shop."

After Sam and I graduated from quirky and trendy dates to traditional ones (movies and ethnic restaurants), we also moved from life stories to our secret transgressions, focusing on romantic relationships. I told him about my behavior with Harvey, how ashamed I was to have kissed him and led him on. Sam dismissed it with a snort. "Nothing," he said (At the time, my revelation felt like a confession, though looking back, I wonder if I told it, in part, because the anecdote also made me appear more desirable). I wanted to tell Sam about how I had lied to Rocky, yet that felt too fresh, too intimate, and too revealing. I winced at the memory of Rocky's face, his dark eyebrows rising and coming together as if in prayer when he asked, "What kind of woman denies she has children?"

Well, my own mother, for one. She married her fourth husband in Vegas without even mentioning us. We were living with my grandmother then, and later when my mother didn't return to claim us—for the ten months her marriage lasted—in foster homes. I wonder if she ever did mention our existence. I didn't tell Sam about any of that. My mother was long dead, no use hunting for pity or making myself appear pathetic. And he came to understand that my childhood was not a time I liked to talk about.

Sam told me of a woman named Natalie whom he had been involved with for nearly two years. He said that after they broke up he couldn't get her out of his mind. He didn't use the word *stalked* (maybe no one used it yet—that could have started with *Fatal Attraction*), though it was the most fitting term for his subsequent behavior. Just to hear her voice, he would call her and hang up (this was when everyone still had landlines) multiple times a week for months. He drove past her house, twenty minutes north of the city in Evanston. More than once, he sat out front, his car idling, in the hope that he would glimpse her walking past a lighted window, ready to peel away if she should spot him.

Sam's affair with Natalie had been passionate. He said that it was the kind of sexual magnetism so powerful that a few times while driving they had to pull over to have sex. Once, right on Lake Shore Drive! I knew I wouldn't tell any of my friends about his confession as it would surely be seen as a giant red flag. *A stalker!* I didn't view it that way. Obsessive and tortured, yes, but he was not stalking with the intent to terrorize or cause harm. I found myself falling in love with him and didn't want to hear any warnings. Besides, I was ashamed that I found myself tremendously jealous of her.

Natalie was married, and for a reason Sam couldn't fully explain, he had pretended to her that he was married as well.

"Maybe so we would be equal in the relationship."

We were lying in Sam's double bed when he told me the story. It was almost 3:00 p.m. on a Saturday. We had woken up around ten but stayed in bed talking and occasionally having sex. "If I couldn't call her at home, why should she be able to call me? I was never in love with her and didn't expect things to go on as long as they did. As sexual as the whole thing was, I didn't want to see her that often. I wasn't obsessed when we were *in* the affair, only afterwards."

I thought about how it might be the perfect time to tell of my lie of omission with Rocky. I found myself too embarrassed. Plus, to be completely honest, I knew there was very little chance of Sam meeting Rocky; they were in such different lines of work. And in the unlikely event they did meet and Rocky did spill the beans, I pictured myself telling Sam, *We only went on a few dates, I don't know why he freaked out when he learned I had kids.*

Yes, there would never again be such a perfect opportunity, but I had been down that perfect-opportunity road once. I closed my eyes at the memory of Rocky silently pushing himself away from the table in the Thai place, leaving me to finish the meal on my own, staring at the golden goddess—holding two types of hot sauce in her lap—in the center of the table, and to pay the check.

"She went crazy when I told her I wasn't married," said Sam. "She stopped speaking to me, wouldn't return my calls—we had a signal: two rings and a hang-up."

"Why did you tell her?" I asked. I scooted against the wall so that my legs went up it as my instructor often had us do in yoga, my heels and ankles pressed against the plaster, giving my calves a good stretch. My legs were slender to begin with, and I really liked the way they looked with all the skin and what little flab I had in those days sinking toward my hips.

"Natalie had started talking about us getting divorces. But she was worried about how it would affect me financially—I had just started my practice and my fictional wife didn't work. I didn't want to marry Natalie, but I thought that after almost two years, the lies, and the damage I had caused her marriage, I owed her. So I decided to come clean and tell her that as soon as she was free, I would be there for her without the cost of a divorce, because I wasn't really married."

His sense of honor touched me.

I spun around and brought my legs back to his bed. I felt sorry for him— his twisted chivalry and the obvious pain he was feeling about what he had done.

"Sometimes it's hard to get out of a lie," I said and put my head on his chest. He had a broad chest with just the right amount of soft, curly hair. He stroked my hair and, in penance for not telling about Rocky, I confessed to a few isolated times I had treated my husband unfairly. My list of marital offenses was surprisingly sparse; probably, I had buried my worst sins so deeply that even I couldn't unearth them.

"Did you buy these sheets?" I asked, looking at the daisy field spread across his mattress, not at all masculine.

"They were cheap but with a good thread count. I didn't know anything about thread count or sheets until Natalie told me how bad mine were. Mostly polyester."

During most of Sam's childhood, his family had struggled financially while his father built his practice. Sam was frugal but liked quality. He started his dental practice seven years before I met him, the ground floor of a large two-flat he bought just west of Ashland before the area became gentrified. He lived on the top floor.

Natalie was a dental equipment rep who invited him out to lunch after a sales call. On the walk back to his office, she took his hand. He was completely surprised—he had noticed her wedding ring—but responded by inviting her up to his apartment. He told her it was a place he kept when he had to work late. He said that he and his wife lived in the suburbs.

"What did Natalie look like?" I asked.

"She was pretty, petite." He paused and squinted as if trying to bring her image into focus. "She had straight, strawberry blond hair—about shoulder-length—and freckles all over. Not really my type. I prefer dark hair, curly or wavy like yours," he said, wrapping a band of my hair around his hand. "But I wasn't seeing anyone at the time. I never expected to hear from her again—and certainly never would have predicted how passionate we would become, how long we would be together, or how I would feel when we broke up."

He turned toward me. He had lovely, full lips—pillowy, soft, though not moist—and large, white teeth, like Chiclets—nice advertising for a dentist, though he wasn't the least bit vain about them. His eyes were large, with heavy lids. He cupped a hand on my right breast. To my displeasure, I immediately pictured a golden idol's breasts, metallic and hard; I winced.

Sam and I had Chinese takeout the night of his confession, a picnic in the field of his flower-printed sheets, planted by Natalie. Over the years we have graduated to a queen mattress, but never a king. We want to be able to find each other at night. That night was when jealousy began. I found myself intensely disliking Natalie: the passion she had shared with Sam, the fact that she had rejected his attempt at making things right, and even her part in the soft sheets fitted on his mattress. And I was jealous of Sam for being able to unburden himself of his sin.

~

Sam and I were married in the basement of city hall two years after we met. We were the oldest couple there that day. A lot of the other brides were pregnant, and more than a few of the other new spouses seemed to be providing American citizenship. We waited with them for our number to be called. A dozen judges had offices along the underground cinder-blocked corridor. When our turn arrived, Mia and Jacob, two of my friends, one of Sam's, his head dental assistant, his mother, and I crowded into a judge's small office.

The longer I was with Sam, the more the memories of my first marriage faded. They seemed of another life, two premature adults set on beginning their careers and raising children. For me it provided the normalcy I didn't have growing up. We had had regular meals every night, entertained other couples on Saturdays, and took two-week vacations yearly. I could remember the scope of it, yet few individual moments stood out. It was a blur of what was expected of responsible couples at the time.

When I did see Don after Sam and I were married, he seemed almost a stranger, a distant colleague with whom I had exchanged shifts for staying up with kids who had the flu or driving them to sporting events.

Sam and I explored new things. We played hide-and-seek (I can remember trembling in my hiding spot under the stairs in his dental office, afraid that he would find me and afraid that he wouldn't). We traveled to places that Don and I would never have considered. Don and I went to Cancún on our tenth anniversary and I pretended to enjoy it; Sam and I visited small villages in Mexico. And for many years, we took turns reading to each other at night. He read mostly history. I read fiction and poetry; like most of the "creatives" at the agency, I had literary aspirations.

I saw Harvey—the gold tits guy—occasionally over the years. He married again, a woman younger than me, and even fathered a baby—at over fifty! Sam and I talked briefly about having a child, but I already had two, was over forty by the time we married, and his disinterest in "rug rats" appeared sincere, though it almost broke my heart whenever I saw how tender he was with his young patients.

Sam and I had what would be considered a good life by any standards. Time moved more like an accordion than the treadmill it had been with Don. How do you sum up so many years? Sam's practice grew. He was always quick to do the latest in dentistry. He had funny sunglasses for his patients so that they didn't have to look at the light fixtures, offered many flavors of dental floss, sugarless lollipops for the children, and for any procedures over two hours he showed movies on the ceiling of his surgery room, which he had constructed on the second floor of his two-flat once we purchased a house. He worked weekends in a lab to develop a more sensitive teeth whitener—less likely to permanently damage teeth—and made a small fortune. When Mia had her first baby, he was at the hospital with me. We had not parented together yet we did grandparent together, an occupation that required less time and drudgery.

I tried to tell him everything, but sometimes it was difficult for me to move a thought from my mind to my lips. I always confessed the embarrassing things—like when I peed while standing in line at Home Depot, too much coffee and a new diuretic, the way pee ran down my leg and formed a small puddle that I simply walked away from; the less tangible things—*the emotionally shameful moments*—felt harder to say. I tried to convince myself that my reluctance had as much to do with modesty as shame, self-revelations being egotistical. How much could a person reveal and still hold onto self? I told myself these things, but I knew I was lying.

Although I rarely went to Sam's conferences with him, I did when, in his late fifties, he was invited to give the keynote at a huge meeting in Boston. I sat in the back row of what must have been a dozen lines of metallic folding chairs and marveled at Sam's confidence and the way all the young dentists looked at him attentively. In the dental world, he was a star.

His talk was the grand finale before the open bar.

"Do we have to go?" I asked.

"Just for a few minutes so I can thank the organizers, say hello to a few people."

In the hotel ballroom, there was a stage with a small band—the kind that plays at Holiday Inns and weddings—and a postage-stamp-sized dance floor that flickered in glowing blue from a disco ball. Most of the dentists were lined up at the appetizer table with tiny paper plates or standing three deep around the bar. No one was on the dance floor. A sad affair. Sam and I made our way toward the bar, stopping every few feet to hear a colleague congratulate him.

My right arm was linked in his left when a short woman, squat really, approached.

"Sam Levy! So wonderful to see you! I don't usually come to these things but when I saw you were on the program, I couldn't resist."

Sam stared at her blankly. Her reddish-gray hair was shaped more or less in a bowl cut, straight bangs in the middle of her brow. Her double chin hung in a soft hammock. Despite her stoutness, the woman wasn't really unattractive—just unnoticeable, the way so many of us become when we age. The pull of gravity and the fading of brightness.

"I'm sorry," said Sam with a kind smile. "But could you remind me how I know you?"

"It's Natalie!" she blurted with a wide grin.

Sam's face paled as he realized who stood before him; my heart fell like an elevator cord had been severed. We both froze as she nattered on.

"I got out of sales right after I knew you, went on to head the division. I'm divorced now." She tilted her head and produced a coy smile. "But I guess you could have predicted that. I've thought of getting in touch . . ."

With the slant of her head, her eyes caught the light in a way that allowed me to imagine how they must have sparkled twenty-five years ago.

After a moment, we were—thankfully—interrupted by two dental students. I stood with a smile plastered on my face, not absorbing a word they said, recalling the jealousy I had once felt toward Natalie. When the students departed, we turned toward the bar; from the corner of my eye, I noticed a flicker on the dance floor. I glanced over to see Natalie—by herself—in the middle of the blue light, languidly swaying to the beat of "Leaving on a Jet Plane." Her arms waved sensually over her head as she strutted slowly from one end of the empty patch of dance floor to the other. Her raised arms pulled her sequined top over her belly, exposing a drooping bulge of white flesh above her pants. Her eyes were closed and her head gently rolled. Did she think herself Salome, performing the Dance of the Seven Veils? Was she envisioning Sam as King Herod? I noticed other people watching, silence growing. A few smirks from the dental students we had just spoken with. Did Natalie believe herself alluring? Did she think she could provoke Sam's obsession once again? I reminded myself that as far as we knew she never knew about the "stalking," only his lie about the fictional wife. Still, she must have remembered their passion. I wondered, did she not know how she appeared now?

The whole room fell silent, mesmerized by her bizarre performance. My long-held jealousy evaporated. No one talked; the only sound in the large crowded room was the band—an occasional screech from the old amplifier. Natalie's head continued to sway. I could see her lips moving to the lyrics:

All my bags are packed, I'm ready to go
I'm standing here outside your door

I thought of some of the things I had kept secret—my quiet sins—and my fascination switched to mortification and then to compassion. I let go of Sam's arm and strode to the dance floor to sway beside her. She opened an eye for a second—perhaps thinking I was trying to steal the show—then closed it again. She was too lost in her head to be bothered. I closed my eyes, took a deep breath and sang along. I tried to make my movements seem silly without mocking her. After an excruciating few minutes, another woman joined us, then a couple more women trickled onto the floor, all imitating what I had tried to establish as an ironically sensual dance. I released my breath. The song ended and the band switched to

"Proud Mary," persuading more people onto the floor to do the fast dances of their own youth, or their parents' youth. Even Sam—an awkward dancer who usually had to be yanked onto the floor at weddings and bar mitzvahs—joined me. He smiled, a closed-lips acknowledgment of my rescue of Natalie, and then twirled around. I thought of the silly abandon with which Rocky and I had danced to the "Monster Mash" all those years ago in that rambling mansion. Then a thought of the possibility of my and Natalie's roles being reversed fleeted across my consciousness—me alone at a conference, Rocky and his wife on the sidelines watching me make a spectacle of myself.

I never saw Rocky again (though I suppose never isn't over yet) and seldom thought of him except when I would see an especially nice photo of a dessert topped with whipped cream, knowing—as he had informed me—that the whipped cream was probably shaving cream so it would not melt under the intense photographic lights.

At the end of that Halloween party as Rocky and I went our separate ways, he had asked, "What are you anyways?"

"Huh?" I had responded, flushed with embarrassment, certain that I had been found out in some way.

"Your costume? What is it? What are you supposed to be?"

After "Proud Mary," Sam and I slipped out of the reception and walked to a small Italian restaurant where the concierge had made reservations for us. We had to walk down a few steps into the cozy dining room, packed with gilded mirrors, twisting plastic vines, gold statues, and twinkling lights. After Sam ordered wine, he reached his hand across the table and cupped mine. He felt proud of me, I knew, because of my rescue of Natalie. I felt like a fraud.

"You know," I said, "after my divorce I lied to one of the first men I dated. I didn't tell him I had children."

"Where is that coming from?" Sam asked. His lips were still full and finely shaped. I had always loved his hooded eyes. He did not yet need glasses except for reading and his lashes had always been longer than mine.

"I was just feeling bad about it." I wanted to set free all my lies and omissions. They felt sealed deep inside. I knew the incident with Rocky was more connected to who I was when I met Sam than who I was now, but I needed to be free myself.

"Everything seemed so important then. What we said or did seemed to become part of our DNA."

"It doesn't matter. You were young and newly divorced, finding your way."

Though I was glad he said it, his absolution did not seem enough. He also needed to recognize the enormity of both what I felt I had done and the fact that I had not told him when he confessed his obsession regarding Natalie that afternoon in his double bed. But my precise explanation would not come. Nor did the fact that Rocky and I actually dated a few more times than I have admitted. And perhaps I led Harvey on a bit more than I've stated.

"I did not feel young."

It suddenly occurred to me that although I know Sam better than I've ever known anyone, there is probably more we don't know about the other than we do know. In what dark crevices do we hide these memories from both ourselves and others? *What are you anyways?*

Despite it all, I *had* been trying to save Natalie from humiliation when I stepped onto the dance floor. No ulterior motive. Maybe that was atonement enough for my sins of omission.

The waiter poured a sample of the wine into Sam's goblet and stood back. Sam swirled and sipped. I glanced at a gilded cherub—each curly lock and tiny toe coated in gold—on a pedestal behind the waiter, and remembered the rumor I had heard many years ago about the girl from *Goldfinger*; it was said that she had died from the gold paint spray blocking all her pores, preventing her skin from breathing and letting the toxins escape. Sam nodded earnest approval to the waiter, and I was struck by how I now—that I had shed just a small swatch of my lies—understood what it felt like not to be trapped inside one's own skin.

Ogden, Ohio

Harvard Thompson returned to town behind the wheel of a boxy, old hearse, hand-painted army green so sloppily that the bristle lines in the brushstrokes showed. He had moved away at the end of our sophomore year in high school to Washington, DC, where his father, a big shot in our town, had received an honorific government appointment. According to my mother, it involved a lot of pomp, but not much substance. A flurry of farewell parties were thrown in Harvard's honor. Tall and handsome, he was indisputably the most popular boy in our class. When he left in 1988, he was clean-cut with a large, toothy white smile and showed promise of being an Ogden High football star. When he returned in the early nineties, his shiny, dark hair hung thick below his shoulders.

There weren't many of us—a few dozen, perhaps—in our age range left in town. Those of us who remained were the would-have-beens, could-have-beens, the losers, and a few people simply taking breaks. I was still there, of course, because of the baby. And Sherrie Holmes had come back to Ohio after her first few weeks of college in Missouri because she was having a hard time breathing in her dorm room. She breathed just fine in Ogden.

We were a shadow community. Not really grown-up, but certainly no longer high school kids. The biggest losers were the ones who still went to the high school kids' parties. Sherrie and I tried to avoid that, which didn't leave us a lot of options. Ogden wasn't much of a town: four blocks of stores, businesses and churches pulled up to the town green like a large hungry family gathered around the table for a free meal. A steep hill descended to the river, which rushed past the junkyard, and a little bar called the Ogden Tavern. The rich people lived above the town, and the poor people below the river, where it sometimes flooded. I had grown up above the river, but now lived below it.

When Harvard came back, it was like the prodigal son returning. We cheered him on as if the hearse was a Cadillac convertible in a ticker-tape parade. Of course none of us actually *saw* him drive into town. Most of us were at our lousy jobs or in our lousy little apartments in the big old houses by the river that had been cut up into rentals. We simply heard about his arrival. But in our minds, we saw him drive down Main Street, smiling his big, toothy grin, casually waving his long, muscular right arm in generous sweeps, amid a shower of streamers and confetti.

They had a big party for him out in the forest preserve that night. I couldn't go because I didn't have a babysitter for Daisy. Usually Sherrie or her mom or Mrs. Fitzgerald, an old woman in the house where I lived, watched Daisy when I needed someone. Sherrie, of course, was going to the party. And we couldn't ask her mom, Mrs. Holmes, or Mrs. Fitzgerald, since partying in the forest preserve was illegal and we didn't want them to know about it. And we didn't have cell phones back then, so they wouldn't have been able to find me in case of an emergency.

So, I tried to study that night. It was pitiful really. I hadn't had much use for school during the last year I attended. I preferred to skip it with T.J. (Timothy, Daisy's father) and go to the forest preserve. Sex was the only way I could leave myself, *leave Ogden*, without actually going anywhere. But almost moments after Daisy was born—or so it seems in retrospect—I craved school. Once T.J. left, I started studying on my own. I went to the library every week and checked out a stack of books. Early in my self-education, I found a thick, old literature textbook, eighteen hundred pages, each page as thin as tissue paper. I renewed that book every week for five weeks, until I had read every poem, every story, and every play in it. I even memorized all the literary terms and elements—*symbol, character, verisimilitude, irony, plot, setting*—since literature was what I imagined I would have studied if I had gone to college. Some of the words were new, some I had learned in high school but they seemed to carry a deeper meaning once I no longer *had* to learn them.

They say reading can be an escape. For me, it was an entry back into a place I had discarded, a connection. I was on track again, heading in the right direction. What I read made me feel tied to something bigger than me.

Usually I liked to have a quiet night at home to study. If I wanted to read in the daytime when I wasn't working, I had to go out to the cemetery. It was the only place with a fence to contain Daisy while I leaned against a headstone and read, Daisy sitting next to me with the few toys I had brought along or stumbling among the graves. But the night of the party for Harvard, the absurdity of my situation gnawed more than usual, so I had difficulty concentrating. I couldn't help but think of them all whooping it up around a big bonfire in the preserve, Harvard regaling them with stories, while there I was, studying for a test that would never come.

Before my parents moved out of town, they had more or less been in the same social circle as Harvard's folks. I remember my mother, a little tipsy, making fun of Harvard's father's DC appointment to my father, laughing in response.

"He thinks he's such a big deal. Can you believe he actually named that boy after Harvard, his *famed* alma mater? The highlight of his life, his glory days." She made a sledding downhill motion with her hand. "All downhill since then. A has-been before he was twenty-one! It's pathetic. The way he slinks around playing golf, barely hanging on until he can collect the principal from his damned trust fund. And now, this silly post."

I remember how she punctuated her distaste by spitting a stream of cigarette smoke into the air after she said it, Bette Davis-style. That, of course, was well before she was diagnosed with emphysema.

The day after the party, Sherrie told me how cool Harvard had become. All the places he had been, and the killer pot (grass we called it back then) he had with him. Harvard probably wouldn't have had much time for her in high school. Sherrie had only been a peripheral part of our crowd. She was pretty, petite with wide blue eyes, and her mother lived above the town, where my parents and most of their friends lived, though unlike them, she lived in a tiny one-story house. But Sherrie hadn't been a cheerleader or a member of the honor society. Her best physical assets, her blue eyes, were reduced and hidden behind thick glasses until she went to college in Missouri and got contact lenses. Her main claim to fame was that she was third flute in the school band, but that wasn't considered a cool or enviable thing. Her mother had been widowed young, a social mark against her in Ogden. I overheard one of my mother's friends saying that women who had lost their husbands weren't as interesting. This seemed cruel to me, also unlikely, though I understood how at that time, everything in adult lives seemed to revolve around couples. When my other friends came home from college for the holidays or breaks, they made disparaging remarks about Sherrie. *I can't believe you hang out so much with Sherrie Holmes.* What did they expect me to do—after everyone else had abandoned me?

"How long is he going to stay in Ogden?" I asked Sherrie.

"Oh, he wants to find a place here, maybe take a few courses over at Burke," she said. She tried to sound casual, as if hanging out with Harvard was no big deal.

I wondered, fleetingly, if his life were so cool why he wasn't in college regularly, and why he wanted to move back to Ogden, a town of slightly more than seven thousand, and attend the community college? Could it be that he was an even sadder has-been than his father—and that sophomore year at Ogden High had been the highlight of his life? (Or, maybe, I actually wondered these things much later, after I knew everything else.)

His return must have taken place in the spring or fall since it was warm enough to have a party in the preserve, but it couldn't have been summer, because none of the college kids were around (I know Daisy was already walking and talking—though not really comprehending; she could just string a few words together). Harvard hung out for a week or so, driving the hearse around town while three or four of the shadow community— though never me—sat in the long back section, the chamber for the coffin, and smoked pot. I wasn't what I would call a good mother, but I was a nervous one. I could picture the headlines of the *Ogden Times*: "Mother Caught in Marijuana Bust."

That would have really sent my parents over the edge. That was another thing that had changed since high school. I cared what they thought. In high school, they had been little more than an impediment to my spending time with T.J. Now that I was willing to do what they wanted, they asked nothing of me. They claimed they were planning to leave town once we all finished high school anyways, that it had nothing to do with my pregnancy. But I had my suspicions. After all, their actual departure took place before I was the first senior at Ogden High to collect my diploma while already showing. I remember, as I smoothed the gown over my belly, how odd it was that the black graduation gowns, with their expanding front panels, seemed made for maternity wear.

Harvard came over to my apartment a few times with the could-have-beens who had latched onto him. He always brought pot and a sixpack and looked at me in such an intense way that it made me avert my head. His stare unnerved me. Even more than his stare, I couldn't get over the fact that he was the most popular boy to walk the halls of Ogden High, and there he was, sitting in my living room. I had been above-average-looking in high school, though far from among the prettiest, yet I had been popular, friends with all the cheerleaders. And until I stopped going to classes, I had earned good grades. But I wasn't a cheerleader or at the top of my class. In sophomore year, Harvard had gone steady with Susan Longman, head cheerleader, who later went to Northwestern University. I was aware that I was prettier than Susan now, had grown into my own. But I had not been Queen of the May. I had only been one of the girls to wear white gloves and a pastel-print dress and dance around the maypole (a custom in Ogden that dated back to the forties), weaving in and out as I held the end of a pink crepe steamer, a little clumsily I might add.

"So, have you heard from Susan?" I remember asking. He sat in the big armchair with frayed arms that I had inherited from a tenant who had moved.

Harvard gave me one of those looks that made me glance away.

"I might drive out to Chicago and see her when she has a break," he said, not really answering my question. Then he remarked on how much Sherrie had changed and asked what I thought of her.

Later, when he was passing a joint among the boys, I studied him and wondered how he would be described if he were a character in a piece of literature. He was handsome in a traditional way, with deep brown eyes, full lips, and the thickest, glossiest hair one could imagine. With it dipping past his shoulders, his hair made him look like an old-time hero, Sir Lancelot or Robin Hood.

Burke Junior College was in Woodville, only about twenty minutes from Ogden. Some of the kids who dropped out of four-year places elsewhere took classes there. There was a small campus and a little strip of bars aspiring to be like the bars in real college towns. Sometimes at night, we would cruise the strip of bars, Daisy in a makeshift bed we had constructed in the back seat (it was before people went crazy over car seats for toddlers) and feel superior to the mothers who left their toddlers on the pavement outside the bars with coloring books. If we had a babysitter, we would go inside a bar for a beer. Woodville was the only place outside of Ogden where Sherrie could go and still manage to breathe. It never occurred to me at the time that she might have had some sort of treatable condition. I hadn't heard of agoraphobia yet. Once we drove the nearly two hours to Cleveland to take Daisy to see Mr. Jingeling at Halle's Department Store and have lunch in the city, like my mother and I used to do, but the minute Sherrie put her foot on the pavement, she began gasping for air, and we had to get right back in the car and drive home. I was disappointed, but couldn't complain since I didn't have a car of my own. Daisy and Sherrie were all I had, and Sherrie took me so many places—the grocery store, the Laundromat—once, all the way out to Kent, where there was a four-year college that had become famous in the seventies for the shootings. At the time, Kent was said to have more bars than any town in Ohio. Driving the streets was like taking a tour of what life was for others our age, a safari of sorts. It was even farther than Cleveland, but we never left the car, so Sherrie was fine.

I don't know how long Harvard had been in town—two weeks—when Sherrie called me in a panic. I had just returned from my weekly trip to the library, where I had shown Daisy the butterflies in the cases in the nature room, along with the arrowheads and chips of pottery found at the burial mound near the preserve. She loved the butterflies, their radiant spread wings.

"You've *got* to get over here," said Sherrie. "You won't believe what's happening with Harvard."

"What, Sherrie? I just walked in the door."

"You have to see for yourself."

"No, please, Sherrie. I'm tired." I looked longingly at the book I had just checked out: *Winesburg, Ohio.* I had asked Hester Lewis, the librarian, to recommend something by a great Ohio author. She had rolled her eyes back in her head—a frequent gesture of hers that made me envisage her mind as a card catalog. Since she was walleyed, it was one of the few expressions that made her eyes appear aligned.

"I have just the book for you," she said when her eyes fell back into place, like mismatched icons in a slot machine.

She walked in her clipped, quiet way, as only a librarian can, to the fiction section and pulled out the book by Sherwood Anderson. I never had an encounter with Hester Lewis (and I had one weekly for years) without wondering afterward why someone with such crossed eyes would choose to be a librarian. Did the words appear double on the page?

"Just get up here, now," demanded Sherrie. "Come in the house the back way."

Then she hung up on me.

I sighed, put the book down on my table, and stuffed Daisy's arms back in the sleeves of her little jacket. After I had walked home from my job at the bakery to collect Daisy from Mrs. Fitzgerald, I had taken her back up across the river to the library, returned home again and settled in with my book; now I was going to have to cross the river again and walk past town all the way up to where Sherrie lived with her mother in my parents' old neighborhood. I just wanted to read my book. I didn't want to walk anymore. I was tired, but there was no arguing with Sherrie when she got this way. I didn't mind living in a lousy little place on the outskirts of town by a polluted river. I just wished that my parents would buy me a car, but I couldn't complain since they already sent me $250 a month to supplement my income from the bakery, because T.J., of course, had skipped out on child support. I accepted the money quietly so I wouldn't need to hear a rant about T.J. Though I knew he had behaved badly, I still felt some loyalty to the passion we had once shared.

"You just missed it!" Sherrie cried when I stepped from her back door into the kitchen.

Mrs. Holmes walked into the room.

"Oh dear, oh dear," she said (she really talked that way) and took Daisy in her arms. Mrs. Holmes was the most maternal and angelic woman I ever knew. As a character in a book, she wouldn't have been believable. She was too nice, too gentle, and too accepting of what life had dealt her. A nimbus almost seemed to glow around her plain but saintly face. Her world was small. She had her garden, and she had her beautiful only child, Sherrie, and she was always happy to take Daisy. But she had no husband and a daughter who could not step a toe outside of Ogden.

"So what's going on?" I asked.

"*Harvard*, he sat here all night, gawking at the house, just staring," said Sherrie, pointing out the front bay window. "On that big boulder at the corner of mother's garden. I could see him from my bedroom window. This morning he was still there and I went out and said, 'Do you want something, Harvard?' and he just kept staring. He didn't answer me."

"You should have told me about him earlier," said Mrs. Holmes. She gently bounced Daisy up and down. Daisy stuck her thumb in her mouth; she was always more babyish around Mrs. Holmes. "Oh dear, oh dear."

"When I looked out this afternoon he *still* hadn't budged from his morning spot, so I told Mother and she called the police," said Sherrie. "Sergeant Wooster came over, but the moment Harvard saw him, he took off through the backyards. He's so fast."

"He's like Charles Manson or something, with all that hair and all that staring," said Mrs. Holmes.

I wanted to say *He's nothing like Charles Manson.* Harvard was tall and handsome, with lush hair. Charles Manson's hair had been all scraggly. But I liked Mrs. Holmes, and my arms were free of Daisy for the time being, so I didn't comment.

"Let's go out and look at the rock," I said.

Mrs. Holmes had the most beautiful front garden, a thick ring of flowers curling around the borders of the yard, encircling a square of emerald grass. The garden was layered in the English style, with hollyhocks shooting up behind carefully orchestrated clumps throughout, flower clusters of varying heights, and painstakingly considered colors. It was one of the few houses in town always guaranteed a spot on the garden tour. The boulder in the far corner served as an anchor. We walked to the rock and stared at it, as if if we looked hard enough the rock would tell us something. Except for a few scuff marks from his shoes, there was no sign that Harvard had been there, until we noticed, at the base of the rock, hidden among the flowered ground cover and purple border flowers, half a dozen crinkled wrappers from packets of Twinkies.

~

After the incident, Harvard's hearse wasn't seen for a number of days, and the gossip died down. What had he really done anyways? Sit on a rock all night and half of the next day, looking at Sherrie's house? To be honest, the whole incident annoyed me a little. If he was going to go obsessing about someone it should have been me. Yes, Sherrie was pretty now that she had exchanged her glasses for contacts and learned about cosmetics; one might even say she was glamorous in a way, with her pouty lips, doll-like eyes, flawless skin, and hennaed red hair. She had been transformed from being on the fringes of the popular crowd, a bit of a washout, to there being rumors among the adults in Ogden that she was promiscuous (Mrs. Fitzgerald told me). I knew they weren't true, but she was a dropout, living with her mom, had no job, and was very pretty, so people were going to talk. And I realize now, though I didn't then, that being fatherless left her more vulnerable to gossip. She was my best friend, yet if I hadn't gotten pregnant and she had been able to breathe in her dorm room, we might never have spoken to each other again after high school. It is hard to explain the hierarchy in a small town unless you have lived in one; it is created from a complicated formula of wealth, appearances, intellect, background, number of years (in some cases, generations) in residence, associations, and the small-town politics that are impossible for outsiders to grasp. And I felt, absurdly (I know now), that even with my single-mother status, I should still be above Sherrie in the rankings, at least of those of us who were left behind.

That night I read half of *Winesburg, Ohio* sitting in my salvaged second-hand armchair, under a pool of yellow light from a floor lamp my parents had handed down to me when they moved. I was amazed that a book with an Ohio setting could be famous. I thought real literature had to take place in Paris or Russia or, maybe, the Deep South. I was thinking about how I would like to write a book like Anderson's some day but it had already been done. In fact, I was thinking that everything had been done, when there was a knock on my door.

It was Harvard. He was dirty, with bits of leaves and twigs snagged in his hair.

"Can I use your shower?" he asked.

"I'm not sure if I have any clean towels."

"Any towel will do," he said.

"Just don't wake Daisy. Her room is right across from the bath."

While I listened to the shower, I wondered if I was harboring a criminal. I had to remind myself that he hadn't actually committed a crime. When he was all dried off and resembling Prince Charming again, I fixed him a sandwich, which he ate on my couch while we talked. I don't think I have ever felt so domestic or maternal, before or since.

"Where's your hearse?" I asked.

"I hid it under branches in the woods," he said as if it made perfect sense. Then he told me a bunch of stories that were clearly untrue—about sailing a ship from the mouth of the Potomac to the Gulf of Mexico, and fighting as a mercenary in a war in Africa. And one story that I believed he *thought* was true, about his mother trying to poison his food during his senior year in high school. I think it was at that moment that I realized he was crazy. But as I was saying, you can't understand the social structure in a place like Ogden unless you have lived there for many years, so it's unlikely that anyone except an Ogdenite would understand how when he began to kiss me, I couldn't stop him. After all, there had never been a more popular boy in the sophomore class in Ogden High's whole history. He was far above me in the pecking order.

He swooped me up and carried me to the bedroom (the first and the last time anyone has done that with me), and undressed me.

The only two people I had made love with at that time were T.J. and Howie Becker. Since T.J. had taken off when Daisy was so young, I didn't have a lot of opportunities for sex after he was gone. I'm not blaming him—he was really little more than a boy himself—in fact, one might even say I was relieved. Having a little girl to care for was more than enough, and we hadn't had much sex since her birth. Howie had only been that once, when he was home on Christmas break and my parents had come and taken Daisy for a few days. Afterward, I had felt foolish and used. So, I wanted to see what sex would be like with someone besides T.J. or Howie.

Harvard pressed his weight down on top of me, kissing, until I forgot everything but the warm, moist commingling flesh of our lips. When I became fully aware of the situation again, I realized that events had taken an odd turn, out of my control. I was like one of the pinned butterflies in the glass cases at the library. At that age and time, I believed that a girl shouldn't appear too anxious the first time she had sex with someone. It was post the period where girls protected their virginity at all costs, though before women realized how much agency they could and should have. Most of us girls still believed we were packages to be unwrapped. So the first time with T.J., I had just lain there, to be admired and ravished. The same was true with Howie. But it was different with Harvard. With T.J. and Howie, I had made myself into the butterfly, curled in a cocoon, waiting to be unfurled, opened up. But with Harvard, he had made me into the butterfly before I had a chance. At some point during our kissing he gradually removed himself while keeping me prone on my bed. He, in fact, had pinned me down, spread-eagle, one foot at one corner, one at the opposite corner, and the same with my hands. I didn't even realize he had arranged my body into an X until he climbed backward out of bed and leaned against the windowsill to smoke a cigarette while he studied me with his eyes. I started to sit up, but he said, "Don't move." He didn't raise his voice, but he spoke with such authority that I remained as still as glass, and thought of the pinned monarch and the blue morpho from Costa Rica, its iridescent blue wings.

You've never really been naked until you've been naked like that.

Technically, I told myself I could have moved; I was not physically restrained, but I felt I had to please him. Still, I knew the situation was not good. I remembered reading how butterflies were pinned directly through their thorax.

Something bad could come of this, I thought.

But nothing bad did happen. A few minutes later, when he returned to bed and we were "doing it," his lovemaking felt so ordinary that I had to keep reminding myself that he was the most popular boy ever in order to remain engaged in the process. It didn't seem real. Afterward, we sat up half the night, smoking cigarettes in bed, discussing our future. He talked about how we would raise Daisy, where we would move, and what it would be like for him being her father. I knew it was all bullshit, but it wasn't in the least unpleasant to hear.

In the morning, he said he was going to go get his hearse and would be back at dinnertime. I never saw him again. And we didn't hear about him again for a week. I never told anyone—not even Sherrie—about that night. The day after I was so tired that I felt like I was walking underwater, sweeping the currents aside to make headway. I had the day off, so I pushed Daisy in her stroller to the cemetery, where I leaned against a tombstone and read more stories from *Winesburg*. I liked the "Hands" story best because I could identify the symbol so easily. *Hands*. I thought of Harvard's hands touching my breasts the night before. If I were to write a book called *Ogden, Ohio*, the night with Harvard might be my first story. I would make his eyes the symbols. Anderson seemed to have the perfect life—writing about Ohio from Chicago. But I had no idea how to go about writing a story, and even if I had, I knew I couldn't use that title. I didn't know the word "derivative" then, but I knew that's what such a book would be.

I am ashamed to say that I fell asleep there in the afternoon sun, and only woke up because Daisy was burying my head in weeds she had ripped up. The feeling of the stems drifting down onto my cheeks had made me dream of butterflies. When I opened my eyes, I noticed that I had failed to latch the cemetery gate. Twice in two days I had been lucky. Harvard hadn't murdered me the night before because of my wayward behavior, and Daisy hadn't wandered off into traffic that afternoon because of my carelessness. I collected my book, positioned her in her stroller, and headed toward my apartment. At home, in the bathroom mirror, I could still see the imprints of pebbles and earth on my cheek from the grave mound where I had rested my head. Later that night, I was relieved that Harvard didn't show up. After Daisy went to bed, I finished the book.

Before this story raises any concerns, I should mention that Sherrie left Ohio and never returned, and I got the education I was after. You could say that I am almost on the other side of learning now (at least in the sense of formal education). I know that my way of looking at literature, its elements, the signs and symbols during my days in Ogden, was a simple, reductive approach. But I remember so intensely how I felt then—staring at those words on the page, as if I looked long enough, I could get inside them and fully comprehend their meaning. It's hard to restrain the feeling of reverence when the terms first pop in my head. When I feel them on my tongue, I often smile with bittersweet recollection. Being on the other side of learning is a little like being on the far side of longing. During my young motherhood in Ogden, I so longed for all the places I would go, all the things I would do and learn, that it sometimes forced me to clutch my belly to stop the ache. Now that Daisy is nearly grown, finished with college, I find myself longing for the past.

Was there ever a moment when I was right in the middle? When just enough was behind me and just enough ahead? If so, I wish I had been conscious enough to recognize the moment. It would have been nice if someone had tapped me on the shoulder and said, "Hey, you're here—take a last look back and a deep breath before moving forward."

Daisy went to Carnegie Mellon. Afterward when she got married in Pittsburgh and became pregnant, I suggested, as a joke, that she name her baby Carnegie. "Good for a boy or a girl," I said. Naturally, she didn't get it. So I guess that would make it dramatic irony, even though I was the sole audience member who could understand my silly little joke.

"Mother, that's pathetic," she said. "Daisy's bad enough, though I suppose that I should just be happy that you didn't name me Candy or Kitty—or some other puerile name. I can't believe you had a baby so young. I would have had an abortion."

When she talks like that, she makes me think that she's my mother reincarnated, which would be impossible since my mother is still alive, though not very, hooked up to oxygen tubes.

But I am getting too far ahead of the story.

I was at the library when I heard that Harvard had been arrested in Illinois. He had gone to Northwestern to see Susan. In fact, he had kept her locked in the basement of an abandoned house near campus for almost two days. It wasn't kidnapping—because she had gone there with him of her own accord, he just hadn't let her leave—but the legal name for it was almost as bad. Forced imprisonment, I think. As soon as I heard the news from my babysitter, Mrs. Fitzgerald, I pushed Daisy's stroller as fast as I could to Sherrie's house.

Sherrie was sitting by herself on the front porch. I went over and plopped myself down beside her, and released Daisy to play in the yard.

"The police were here just an hour ago to tell us that Harvard had been apprehended. Did you hear that the hearse was stolen?"

The word *apprehended* sounded unnatural on her tongue.

"I only know that he got arrested for holding Susan," I said.

"The funeral home where he stole it didn't miss it right away because they didn't use it anymore. It was in an old garage back behind the place. Harvard got a new battery for it before he painted the hearse green."

"You're kidding," I said. It was just an expression. I knew she wasn't kidding.

"That's not all. You haven't heard the worst part yet. *Harvard came here after escaping from a mental institution!* Well, not actually escaping, he was on a weekend pass and the paperwork somehow got messed up so no one realized it until he was gone for over a week."

"They have passes from mental institutions? Kinda lax," I said. But my mind was elsewhere, marveling at the fact that I had actually had sex with a guy on the run from the law.

"*Kinda,*" she repeated sardonically. "They said they weren't at liberty to say what was wrong with him. But they said it was nothing for us to be concerned about. Besides, he's in custody. My mother said that if it was the type of illness where he could get a weekend pass it probably just started as a nervous condition. Our neighbor, Mr. Greer, said that after what he had done with Susan, they should throw away the key. Mom told him that Harvard deserved our sympathy."

I wasn't really listening anymore because I was thinking about the stolen hearse, what a bad paint job Harvard had done, and how impossible it would probably be for them to restore it to its natural state. And how if it hadn't been green—if it had been black as it should have been—I might have recognized it for the obvious symbol of foreboding that it was.

"Too bad he didn't come back here, it would be kind of exciting to watch the cops make the arrest," said Sherrie. "Liven Ogden up a bit."

"Uh-huh," I said, and called out to Daisy, who had just curled her pudgy little hand around a hollyhock stem that must have looked as tall as Jack's beanstalk from her perspective, "don't you dare think about breaking that flower stem! Mrs. Holmes won't let you play here anymore."

In actuality, I knew Mrs. Holmes would never be so vindictive. Besides, I didn't really care whether or not Daisy was allowed to play there. My mind was already drifting away from Ogden, imagining my own adult-sized beanstalk—thick, green tendrils woven together—shooting magically from the earth, and how I knew it was not going to appear, that I was going to need to find my own way out. I don't think it was at that moment that everything changed. Many moments of revelation followed. But it is a moment I have etched deeply in my memory, down to every detail, including Daisy's eyes as she glanced in my direction, still clutching the stem, daring me.

Noir

I sat at the old desk we found years ago at a junk store, sorting bills under the glare of the gooseneck lamp, deciding which ones to pay online and which to send in the mail. It felt like a balancing act, though in actuality the two or three days it took an envelope to reach its recipient didn't give me any real advantage. It made me feel better to imagine their slow journey. I had never before been one to worry about money, so having some sort of process made it less onerous. I made one stack of envelopes, then another and then a third, before shifting bills back and forth between piles, deciding based on necessities, late fees, and what we wouldn't miss if it was shut off.

My wife, Mary, entered the alcove that we had elevated (in name) to home office, dressed for a run—my oversized hooded gray sweatshirt and her neon-green leggings. In headlights, she always looked like a pair of torso-less running legs; we used to laugh at that. Did the visibility of the bright color really make her safer, or could the severed legs cause a driver to panic and run into her?

She handed me a sheet of notebook paper.

"Take a little dictation," she said. After speaking, her mouth quickly returned to the unforgiving line that had divided her nose and pointy chin for months.

I placed the paper flat on the desk surface, between bill stacks, and said, "Okay, go."

"*I can't take it anymore. No one is to blame. I leave everything to my wife.*"

I scrawled quickly.

"That it?"

"Sign your full name."

I scribbled my name as I was preparing to do on checks, folded the sheet in half, and handed it back to Mary. I suspected the request to be some sort of test that I would immediately fail if I questioned her about it too soon.

"I should be back in forty," she said and was gone.

I wanted to ask, *forty years? Forty days and forty nights?* A joke, but given the way things were between us, I knew neither of us would laugh. We used to laugh all the time; you could say that was our thing: laughter. Even weak jokes; in fact, we thought they were particularly funny. We laughed when we talked on the phone, when we traveled, when we made love, even when we said our vows. We laughed when we watched the old black-and-white films that we both loved. We laughed when we fought, when we called each other names. We laughed at how ugly we could get, at how stupid and mean people could be. She sometimes called me "One to laugh in the face of danger," Mary being the danger. I thought of her as slightly off, a bit maniacal in her laughter—as she was with her humor. But I didn't tell her that. It was how she had gotten by during a difficult childhood. In the long run, no one was more competent and stable than she.

And the thing was, we totally got each other.

That was before the girl, Risa, got sick. We always called her "the girl" or "our girl" until she was diagnosed with a rare syndrome that the doctors said was similar to Fabry disease. After that, she became Risa, her given name, which felt like a dark irony since we had once found her name—meaning sea nymph or laughter—slightly comic. We became more and more solemn with every bit of news regarding Risa's condition: that she would have some hearing and vision loss, that her skeleton would not form fully or evenly, that her head could become larger than normal, and that she would have lifelong bouts of pain in her hands and feet. Eventually her kidneys could give out. We grew slightly hopeful to learn that the disease would not affect her intelligence and that, with proper care, she could live into her forties, maybe longer. She would be able to experience life, maybe travel the world, but probably not outlive her caretakers.

During the learning stage, our only big laugh came when we were told her medications would cost over $100,000 a year. Of course we laughed—dark, bitter spasms—it was absurd. Mary talked of burglarizing the drug-store. I enjoyed seeing her smile at the idea of assembling an all-black cat burglar getup. Her scheming felt like old times. She said we could sell the other drugs we got in our haul. It would be too obvious if we only took Risa's meds. Though the episode restored our familiar feeling of laughter, our plans could not withhold the weight of reality; even if we didn't get caught, we couldn't rob the store every month.

In the year since, we turned into people we didn't recognize. Or at least Mary did.

"Daddy? Where's Mommy?"

Risa stood in the doorway to the home office, the exact spot Mary had been moments earlier. Like her mother, Risa's face was pale, except for a spatter of light freckles across her nose, with delicate features scrunched in the center of her face. She inherited Mary's fair coloring, her wavy, ginger hair. But she had my round face, dimpled chin, and dark eyes, and shortly after the diagnosis her eyes became underscored with the same shadowy bags I have had since childhood. The pouches would have concerned me if I hadn't had them all my life; instead they connected us and gave her face an odd maturity. Risa's head looked disproportionally bigger than her torso—a bit like a Charlie Brown character—but I wasn't sure I was imagining that, given what I knew could happen, plus her nightgown was so wispy. I reminded myself that all five-year-olds have to grow into their heads. I left the desk to squat beside her.

"Just out for a run," I said, wrapping my arm around her waist. Her breath felt warm on my face, smelled milky. "Does something hurt?"

"No, I'm okay. I just felt one of you go out."

That was the way she talked now. She never heard or saw anything. She felt it.

"Do you want me to read you a story?"

She nodded. I scooped her up and carried her to the living room where we snuggled together in a large armchair upholstered in cat fabric, representative of Mary's cat stage—as were the three live cats we housed and fed. How much could we save without shelling out for cat food and litter? I picked up the book that I had left spread open on the arm before I had carried her to bed.

"No, don't read one; *tell* me a story—about you and Mommy."

I told the one about the first time Mary invited me to dinner and how she served water soup. I dislodged myself from our chair to stand and act out the flourish with which Mary placed the large bowl of steaming clear water in front of me before sitting down to her own bowl across the table. Though she had heard the story many times, Risa squealed. I mimicked Mary: *Is yours okay? Enough salt?* I mimicked myself salting the water. Risa threw her head back in giggles.

Both our heads turned at the sound of the front door opening. The new, grim Mary entered, only to break into a smile when she spotted Risa with me sunk in the chair.

"What are you doing up?" She lifted Risa and carried her off to bed, stroking Risa's hair with her free hand, without even looking at me.

We had both been angry at the diagnosis, but Mary had redirected her wrath at me when I quit my job. Dazzles, where I worked, was outwardly sympathetic about Risa, but as the year wore on, they began to see me as the person they could make do anything, the person who could not quit no matter what they threw my direction. I was supposed to be general manager, but on the night two waiters and the dishwasher didn't show, Henry, the owner, said, *Sorry, you drew the short straw.* I thought Mary would be proud of me. She was the bigger earner, the one with the health insurance. She always liked to say—only half in jest—*Young man, I like your spunk!* My salary was like a drop in the proverbial bucket. But she was not amused. She had screamed *You what? You what? Your job pays for half her medication!* The other half was covered by insurance.

"It's a shitty job, getting worse every day," I had said. "I can find another, a place where they won't know about Risa."

In the past, Mary would have wanted the details, a description of the look on Henry's face when I walked out. We would have found it hilarious. Now, all she cared about was the medication and the fact that by quitting I had blown my chance for receiving unemployment. Of course, in the past I would have told her before I quit. Even if I hadn't known the exact moment that would trigger it, I would have warned her it was going to happen. I found another job that paid only slightly less within the month. Still, whatever strands had been holding us together were further frayed.

Mary returned to the living room and sat on the couch opposite the cat chair and crossed her brilliant green legs. Measles, our black cat with one speck of white on his tail, pounced into Mary's lap. I thought that maybe we should not have named our cats after illnesses—Measles, Typhoid, and Mumps—but didn't say it aloud. Surely, the same thought had crossed Mary's mind. A harbinger of sorts. Maybe not, the cats were years older than Risa. Mary stroked Measles and eyed me. The youngest of seven children, a big Irish Catholic family, Mary had not been allowed pets because of the cost of care and feeding, though there had been a mean outdoor tom to scare away rats that Mary considered her own. She told me she spent hours coaxing lumps out of that cat's fur. Mary loved the silky feel of our indoor cats.

"So, aren't you going to ask about the note?"

"I could see what it was. A suicide note," I said, and then, trying to affect a gangster accent, added, "I'm worth more dead than alive."

Mary didn't laugh.

With the diagnosis, we had both taken out unusually large amounts of life insurance for people in their early thirties. After a year on the policy, a deadline we had just passed, we could even collect in the event of suicide, though an accident would be more profitable.

"I've always wondered how those men who killed their wives and then pretended it was suicide got their wives to write the fake notes," she said. Along with our love of noir films, Mary is an aficionado of true crime. "Turns out it is much easier than I thought. Though don't worry, it was just a joke—to see how you would react or whether you would ask any questions."

Mary watches every one of those reality murder shows. She has drawn me into watching them as well, though not with her zeal. They used to fascinate her, sometimes amuse her. *How in the world did that tiny woman get her husband into that suitcase and out to the pier; someone had to have helped her. Seems like you can poison anyone over sixty and get away with it—no autopsy once you hit that age. Why would anyone not just get a divorce; child support ends at eighteen. These people are all so stupid to believe that in this day and age with DNA and so many types of forensics they could commit a perfect crime.* Since Risa's diagnosis, the shows made her angry. The fact that people could waste other people's perfectly good lives for no real reason. She still liked the old noir movies—maybe because unlike the ugly true stories, the actors were glamorous.

Mary's phone buzzed. She pressed it to her ear.

"Hi, Em," said Mary. "Yes, she's fine."

Mary rose and walked into the alcove to talk.

I remembered that she had not told me that the soup was water—and only water—until we had been seeing each other for over a month. She had called that a joke as well, but I knew that—as with the note—she had been testing me, to see what I could take. She had been let down a lot in her family. Never anything but hand-me-downs. Very little attention from her parents. Her father had a drinking problem, would sometimes disappear for days. Her next youngest sibling was five years older than she; the rest were closer to each other in age, only a year or two apart. She felt left out of their antics. Bullied sometimes. No money left for Mary for college. She had been tested with every decision her family made, and had turned into a tester, usually a playful one, able to get away with saying "it was just a joke." Yet, somehow, the note felt more serious. The fact that she told me not to worry worried me. Plus, she had not been playing many jokes for the last year.

Unlike Mary, I had a privileged—though not over-the-top—childhood. Only one sibling, a younger sister, Stephanie. College had been expected and delivered to both of us. I earned respectable grades though did not distinguish myself. When I became a waiter after college, my parents didn't complain. When I was still a waiter five years later, they offered suggestions but didn't interfere, said the important part was obtaining the education not using it to make money. When I moved up in the ranks to an assistant GM, they behaved as if I had been nominated for the Supreme Court. They liked Mary but didn't fully approve of the fact that she had never attended college, only a few noncredit business courses. I don't know what they thought of the fact that she had ascended the culinary ranks, leaving the actual restaurant where we both started as servers to climb the corporate ladder. She oversaw three high-end restaurants now, two in Chicago where we lived and one in New York where she traveled once or twice a month. When she focused her sometimes manic behavior on an objective, she usually achieved her goal.

"Em is coming down," said Mary, as she shoved her phone in her back pocket.

Em lived on the top floor of our three-flat. Her rent and that of the two guys below us paid the mortgage.

Mary bought the place the year we met. How had she saved so much as a waitress? *Stole it*, she said, *just joking*. Was she? She was the only person I knew in our midtwenties who owned a house, a building in fact. She was so much more motivated than I. Funny and ambitious and lovely with her fair Irish looks. And I loved the way she dressed, in vintage clothing arranged like it was an ensemble created by an exclusive modern designer. Fur collars. Silky blouses. Jackets with shoulder pads. Fascinators tilted on her head. She had created a stylish look before she actually had money to pay for it. My parents were nuts to think Mary had gotten the better end of the deal. If Risa hadn't been born, I might not have even accepted the promotion from waiter to assistant GM. Being a waiter, having a few drinks at the bar after closing, suited me fine.

I thought of asking Mary to return the suicide note now that I had passed the test, but I couldn't find the right tone to strike before Em knocked on the door. That was how bad things had gotten between us— that I couldn't simply ask. Or maybe I thought the test wasn't over.

As was her habit, Em entered without waiting for one of us to let her inside. Our door was always unlocked. The door opened into a hallway with stairs up to Em's and down to the guys' apartment, next to the outside door which was always bolted.

A few years older than us, Em already lived in the building when Mary bought it. An attorney, Em would probably have left to buy her own place if Mary hadn't arrived. They became fast friends. They were both ambitious and hardworking, though Em's countenance was quieter. She wore plain suits for her position at work and crew sweaters and jeans for hanging around the house. Mary's ginger hair fell in wide waves past her shoulders, while Em's white-blond hair was cut perfectly straight at chin level. Her features were bolder than Mary's, pretty in a firm rather than delicate way. She wore glasses with clear rims on the bottoms and dark lintels across the tops, like an extra set of eyebrows; they looked like old-maid specs to me, but Mary assured me they were expensive and stylish. And despite the glasses, Em had the type of look that women have in optical ads; the glasses did not become part of her face, rather her face served as a vehicle to model them.

After dealing with dull tax laws all day, Em was a perfect audience for Mary's humor, but didn't seem to get mine. Naturally, I hadn't liked Em at first; I felt we competed for Mary's attention. But when Risa was born, she was there for all of us equally, plus a built-in sitter. And when Risa got sick and Mary hardened after I quit my job, she was there for me.

"Scrabble anyone?" In offering, Em held out her old, maroon game box, all the corners broken so that the top didn't fit snuggly and she had to clamp the bottom in place on the ends with both hands. With the three of us, it was always old films or games.

Mary and Em set up the board and letter racks while I made us tequila and cranberry–apple juice cocktails, using the thick, blue glasses we had bought in Mexico on our honeymoon. It was a Sunday night. Monday and Tuesday were my days off at the restaurant. Such is the restaurant business for those on the ground. It was a work night for Mary and for Em, so she would stick to one drink. Risa had kindergarten, a full day. My turn to get her up and ready, but I could always go back to bed after I dropped her off. We sat cross-legged around the coffee table to play. I seldom won, but I liked the fact that some of the tension between Mary and I dissolved when it was the three of us focused on the game. The first four letters I picked were *S*, *I*, and two *U*'s, which reminded me of the word *suicide*. I considered mentioning the note, telling Em about the "joke," a guarantee that Mary could never use it. I quickly scolded myself—*Mary would never use the note*. It was a test from a woman with a very sick daughter whose birth family had failed every test that had ever arisen. To mention the note in Em's presence would be a betrayal that would ensure my permanent place on the list of those who had failed her.

On her first turn, Mary scored big with the word *adz* on a triple letter square. It had taken me at least a dozen games to realize that winning was more dependent on strategy than vocabulary. College had failed me there. I could have done *pursuit* and scored reasonably well with the four point *U* on a double letter. Instead I did *up*, the double-point square remaining barren. I was hanging on to three letters that could be used in *suicide* in case I picked the others. If I put the word on the board it would be unnatural for me *not* to mention the note. I practiced how I would say it in my head: *Funny I would get that word. Suicide.*

My phone vibrated during Em's turn. My parents calling.

"I should take this," I said. It turned out they were calling to make me an offer of paying for the three of us to go to Disney World during Risa's spring break; that was almost six months in the future, but they said that to get good rates, they needed to book now. This was a big deal, since I knew they were also investing for Risa's college. Plus, they helped out with large checks on our birthdays and holidays.

Mary's face transformed at the news. A huge smile.

"Really? That's great! Florida in March. Will we be staying with them?"

Disney World was not the sort of vacation my parents had ever planned when Stephanie and I were children. They liked educational trips, like DC and Gettysburg. They had moved to Florida a few years ago, less than an hour from Orlando, but talk of Disney World had never come up before now. I have to say it wasn't exactly what Mary and I would have chosen for a vacation either. But everything had changed with Risa's illness.

"They only expect us to stay with them a few days. The rest of time they're putting us up at a Disney Hotel on site, so we won't need to drive to the grounds every day."

"Wow."

~

Looking forward to a future trip changed our lives more than I ever would have guessed. We were laughing again. When I called the hotel to check on something in our room, the Disney World operator had repeated and confirmed our names by saying *Carl with a C as in* Cinderella, Mary *with an* M *as in* Mickey, *and* Groff *with a G as in* Goofy. Mary cracked up when I told her. We talked that way whenever we could. *Do you want to go out to dinner tonight, dinner with a D as in* Donald Duck? Em joined in on the game, and Risa tried, though she could only spell a few words and didn't know all the Disney characters.

I completely forgot about the suicide note. There was no way Mary would kill me and take Risa to Disney World on her own. Of course, I knew there was no way *period*.

The dynamic between the three of us grown-ups changed as well. While it had first been me and Mary, then Mary and Em, then the three of us, and then Em and me, it was back to Mary and me, with Em at the outskirts of our acute triangle. I was glad not to need Em so much. Nothing had happened between us—not really, just the way she had touched my hand and removed her glasses on a night she joined Risa and me for dinner once when Mary was in New York. There had been something in the touch, in the way our eyes connected and hers seemed to say: *I am here for you in any way you need.* I tried to return her gaze with a look that said: *I need you.* But we both agreed, without a word, that we would not hurt Mary. I realized when she went up to her place that the most serious tests were often the secret ones that only the test taker or giver knew about. I didn't see the tacit offer as a betrayal on Em's part. Em was there for both of us. Besides, I would not have pursued it, even when Mary and I went for weeks without sex and she scoffed at the attempts I made at reconciliation. But once the dynamic shifted with word of the Disney trip, I sensed that Em felt a little left out. I tried to include her more but saw that any special attentions only made it worse, as if I pitied her.

Noir

~

We had a scare about a month before the trip when Risa showed extreme signs of fatigue, broke out in rashes on both her arms, and needed to pee so frequently that she wet her pants at school. A near-mortal embarrassment to her, but she was a trouper, never complained. After a series of tests and a week of bed rest, the docs verified we were good to go. It was Risa's second trip to Florida, but she didn't remember the first one. We bought her a miniature plane in an airport gift shop, and the flight attendant gave her a small, faux-brass pin with wings. My parents babysat Risa one of the nights we stayed with them so that Mary and I could go out to dinner and dancing. *Dancing!* We hadn't done that since before Risa was born. Mary wore an amber-colored dress from the forties with a wide belt, a swing skirt, and sequins sprinkled across the deep neckline. We got home in the wee hours and made love on the bathroom floor, since we were sharing my parents' guest bedroom with Risa. We laughed and laughed—even more because we had to hold the noise inside—as we slid on the fuzzy baby-blue bathroom rug and maneuvered our tangled bodies between the avocado-colored sink and the old, matching bathtub, a human cruise ship coming into port. The next morning, my parents took Risa to play miniature golf so we could sleep in. Before they returned, I got up and made us Bloody Marys.

Our hotel was magnificent in its campiness. Even better, my parents had gotten some sort of special pass from a Disney executive in their gated retirement community that allowed us to skip most of the long lines. It seemed that everything was in Technicolor—both the exhibits and the real skies above. Risa loved the Mad Tea Party and "it's a small world." And she found Ariel's Grotto so enchanting that we went through three times. We took a photo of her sitting on the giant half-shell throne beside Ariel in her shimmery-green fishtail. Risa gasped at lunch when we told her that her name had something to do with being a sea nymph.

"Maybe I'll grow up to be a mermaid!" She looked down at her pale twig legs in her tiny shorts as if she might be able to see scales forming.

The first night Risa was too tired for the parade and fireworks, so we put her to bed after dinner; Mary and I—arms linked around each other's waists—watched the colorful explosions from our hotel room window, knowing as we stood together that we would do anything for each other, and that the two of us would do anything for Risa.

Noir

At the pool in the late afternoon of the second day, we took turns splashing with Risa in the kid's pool. When she found another girl to play with, we sat on the side making up stories about the other hotel guests. Which couples were having affairs—*who would bring his mistress to Disney World?* Which families were happy? Which were wealthy and which took out a high-interest loan to bring their five children to Disney World? Except for a few calls Mary had to take about the New York restaurant, it was the perfect afternoon. By the third day, we had grown weary of the perky voices of all the Disney employees, but not of Risa's excitement. We continued taking rides until it was time to head for the airport. All three of us were exhausted when we boarded the plane. A man behind Risa's window seat hacked a phlegmy cough, so after she got to watch takeoff from the porthole, I traded my aisle seat with her so she would be as far away from the sick man as possible. Mary wrapped a thin scarf around Risa's nose and mouth. Naturally, she needs to be particularly careful about catching colds.

We were thrown back into our old lives full force. I woke the next day with a sore throat and my ears occluded but had no choice except to go into work after being off a week. Mary got a call about some problems in New York, so she needed to fly back out the night after we returned. The second day after our return, a Saturday, Mary still in New York, my head so clogged I could barely see or hear, Em came down to babysit while I drove blindly into the restaurant. It was the day we opened the outdoor patio for spring and summer—there was no calling in sick.

When I returned home, Em greeted me at the door, a slip of paper in her hand.

"What the fuck is this?" she demanded.

She handed me the paper and made a gesture of shoving her glasses up her nose (though they had not slipped down), then knotted both fists on her hips and glared at me.

I looked at the message on the paper. Given the severity of my cold, it took me a moment to assimilate and focus.

I can't take it anymore. No one is to blame. I leave everything to my wife.

Carl Groff

"Where did you find this?"

"Where do you think? Where you put it. Under the lining in the medicine cabinet."

"What were you doing looking under the lining?"

"I was grabbing Risa's meds—not that *how* I found it has anything to do with it. *Carl, what the fuck were you thinking?*"

Em could be a bit proper. I had never heard her say *fuck* two times in rapid succession.

I must have had a temperature well over a hundred. My ears were so clogged I could barely hear, and with every breath I felt like I was inhaling glass shards. I thought of explaining, but that seemed unfair to Mary, given how well everything had gone in Florida. Plus I wasn't coherent enough to tell the story in a way that made sense.

"It was a really bad time. In fact, I completely forgot about the note." I laughed weakly. "Plus, I have a lot of life insurance."

All three statements were true.

"You *asshole*," she screamed. She grabbed the note back from me and ripped it in half, then into fourths, then eighths. "I have half a mind to tell Mary. But she has enough on her plate. Don't you *dare* think of doing this again. Ever."

She crumpled the scraps into a ball.

"You go to bed," she said, her voice regaining normal pitch. "I'll be down in the morning to take Risa until Mary gets home."

Taking the note with her, Em slammed out of the apartment. I took a double dose of cough syrup with codeine. I barely pulled off my clothing before I fell into bed, trembling from chills. I didn't wake until Em stuck her head in our room in the morning to tell me that she and Risa were off to the park and that Mary called to say she would be back from New York in the late afternoon. I staggered to the bathroom, drank straight from the cough syrup bottle and returned to bed clasping it. I left the syrup on the bedside table in case the feeling of a glass-shard-lined throat returned. I slept through the day until it was nearly dark outside.

I awoke to find Mary sitting on the side of the bed, wearing her short swing car coat, driving gloves, and a feathery fascinator hat—festooned with a tiny veil—clamped at an angle on the right side of her head.

"Risa and I went out for pizza with Em."

"How was New York?" I croaked.

"Horrible. It looks like we are going to have to close the New York place."

I knew that was the corporation's main moneymaker.

"I'm so sorry." My response sounded weak, unsympathetic or unaware of the severity of this action, but it was all I could muster.

"I'm going to sleep on the couch so I don't catch this. In the meantime, I made you this concoction. Sit up."

She held a tall water glass containing a substance that glowed an unnatural red in the light that leaked in from the bedroom door. I pulled myself up to lean against the headboard and took the tall glass from her outstretched hand.

"What is it? Radioactive Kool-Aid?"

"Flu medicine mixed with cough syrup, perfectly safe." I glanced at the cough bottle and saw that it was nearly empty. I couldn't remember how much the bottle contained the last time I took a swig. I drank half the concoction down without stopping. It had a sickly sweet metallic taste that felt good on my throat. I remember how Mary told me that as a girl she learned not to drink milk at dinner if it appeared in a pitcher. If not poured straight from a carton or bottle, it meant her mother had made the milk from powder to save money. She said the artificial milk had a terrible chalky taste.

I tried to hand the glass back to Mary.

"Finish it," she said.

I swallowed the rest. She took the glass from me and placed it on the table beside the empty cough syrup bottle. I sank back down beneath the covers. Mary rose and walked to the door. As she stood in her heels, silhouetted in the light, she looked—with her fancy hat—like a femme fatale in a movie from the forties.

"I love you," she whispered.

"Me too," I said.

Within seconds, sleep began to wash over me—heavy, liquid dreams mixed with distorted shadows cast by the bedroom furniture—and words I needed to say that I couldn't bring to the surface of my consciousness. *What, what, what?* Then, amid my dreamscape of mermaids, talking furniture, and swirling teacups, I remembered. I needed to tell Mary that the suicide note was gone, ripped to tiny pieces; I struggled but couldn't roust myself. Then I felt a gentle surge of relief as the memory of Em finding the note floated within reach: Em was a witness; she might even have saved the scraps; she could vouch for the fact that I had been suicidal. But a mistake—an accidental overdose—would be even better. I tried to push myself up; I needed to tell Mary. They couldn't know she poisoned me! The next thing I knew was darkness, complete extinction. I doubt I have ever gone so deeply under before, so far beneath the surface that I was surprised when my eyes opened to the gray light of morning to find myself alive. Mary could have committed the perfect crime, but hadn't. Oddly, I did not feel I had passed her test, I felt she had passed mine. All I needed to do was get up and start another day, where the girl would have us both.

Her Life in Parties

And what costume shall the poor girl wear to all tomorrow's parties?
—"All Tomorrow's Parties,"
LOU REED, *Velvet Underground*

Andrea had mistimed her arrival. Only a half dozen people were scattered about the large room that Ethan had rented above Romano's for his book party. After a lifetime of attending parties, over fifteen years as an adult, she should have been able to get it right. Instead she was early, forced to join a twosome of the other unfashionably early: a young woman and Ethan's friend, Will. Her entire attraction to them was that they had been the first people to make eye contact with her. She was stuck nodding and smiling until a better option presented itself, despite the fact that they probably wished she would disappear even more than she wished she could.

"I'm the type of guy who likes to follow through on whatever I start, no matter how hard," explained Will to the young woman—what was her name? —and it was all Andrea could do to keep from rolling her eyes. The type of man who had to go around explaining what type of man he was generally had no idea who he was, and on the rare occasions when his proclamation did bear a resemblance to truth it was usually in direct opposition. How many tightwads had told her of their generosity? How many men said they loved to read but never seemed to talk about any books besides the ones they would have been assigned in high school or the first year of college? And how many men liked to present themselves as feminists but couldn't stand to see a woman get ahead? In fact, it was Andrea's theory that you could accurately assess most men simply by assuming they were the opposite of who they claimed to be.

"What was the last thing you finished that you initially thought was too difficult?" Andrea asked brightly of Will. He looked at her and smiled but didn't respond, yet his quiet brown eyes offset his boastfulness. His nose had been broken more than once. Andrea had only met him a few times previously, but apparently, he was the type guy who didn't walk away from a fight. Still, he—smartly—did not respond to her bait. Will turned back to the young woman, as if Andrea had said nothing. She didn't mind. Perhaps her wish had come true and she had disappeared, become invisible.

The young woman hadn't so much as acknowledged her question. Andrea felt like telling her to relax; they weren't competing. She had no interest in Will. Instead she used the moment of invisibility to study the younger woman's face, a perfect square of pore-less pale skin under a patina of faint-pink freckles. Her eyes were blue and her lips pink. Her coloring made Andrea think of sherbet. The woman was younger than Andrea had first guessed, twenty-five perhaps, the same age she had been when she met Ethan, at a party no less. That was back when—as she was dressing and applying her makeup—she believed a party could change her life.

At *this* party, she had only two objectives: to congratulate Ethan on the success of his book and to make it through a few hours without looking lost or foolish or—or, more importantly, that she could care less that he had dumped her. Ethan was on his way to being a star. There was no point in resenting his success, resenting his breaking it off with her—it was just his good fortune that he managed to do it right before the book sold so he didn't come off as a cad. He was a talented man, a nice man, who deserved his good fortune. He didn't owe her a relationship, and he had made the split as kind as possible under the circumstances. She was right to congratulate him and try not to alienate him. She wasn't expecting anything. Just two hours of celebrating his success, and then she could leave.

Andrea took a sip of her Blue Moon and surveyed the room. It had taken her years to make the shift from fancy-girl drinks to beer, and she was still proud of the change. It meant she could nurse one or two glasses all night (two hours in this case) and be less hungover in the morning. The pale beer and the fresh orange slice tasted invigorating. She licked the foam from her lips. Ethan stood in the back by a table piled high with his books, engaged in an intense discussion with the man unloading them from boxes. This was a party of his friends. Didn't Ethan know it was wrong to sell books here? That was for parties thrown by publishers and bookstores. It wasn't that he was cheap—the party would cost more than the small percentage made off each book. It was the concept. Andrea checked herself. That was just the sort of thing that had gotten her in trouble during their relationship, letting him know about such social faux pas. She would show herself to be above that now—buy two books.

"I've never been to a book party before," said the young woman. "Are you supposed to bring presents?"

It took a moment too long for Andrea to realize that the woman was addressing her, not Will.

"Oh, definitely, usually something huge. It's like having a baby or getting married." Both Will and the woman stared at her. Andrea laughed a little too loudly. "Just kidding. No, no gifts. At least, there isn't any etiquette one way or the other."

~

At Andrea's first party on her sixth birthday, she hadn't realized that people would actually bring gifts. Before the party, she had only received presents from her family. When she first understood that the brightly colored packages being carried down the stairs to the basement where her mother had set up two card tables covered with pink crepe paper were for her, she had been beside herself, thrown into a mad frenzy. She was unable to make it down the stairs without sitting on a step and ripping open the box from a little boy whose name she couldn't recall. She was amazed to find a complete set of plastic doll dinnerware, six brand-new matching plates and bowls, saucers, and tea cups all neatly arranged in slits in the cardboard packaging. *These were for her!* All of these children were bringing boxes of things her mother would not have relented to purchase when there were so many hand-me-down toys—mostly with broken or missing pieces— laying about. How could something normally so difficult suddenly become so easy? Her mother had tried to drag her down the stairs so the other children and mothers didn't need to walk around her but she was overcome—perhaps for the first time—with the fever of greed. It hadn't been easy, being the youngest of four girls.

~

Andrea glanced at Ethan. The intense discussion with the man unloading the boxes had turned into an argument. That was one thing about Ethan; he had never claimed he *didn't* like to argue. In fact, he had said he thought a person should argue when he thought he was right. Her heart lurched. Was he the only man who was who he said he was? Then she reminded herself that just because he thought he was right didn't mean that he *was* right.

A group of young women from Ethan's office entered, laughing and teetering on their extra-high high heels in a tight knot, all their chins facing the direction of the bar, reminding Andrea of a gaggle of geese. Andrea knew two of them. They were always full of gossip. They would provide a far better harbor than Will, whom she barely knew, and the sherbet girl, who still seemed to believe they were competing for Will's attention.

"Excuse me," Andrea said to Will and stepped across the space to the women who had gathered at the bar. Parties always create their own landscapes, she observed. At least for her, they did. This one currently seemed a field, and she had just crossed a tiny creek from a small grove to a mountain covered with a flock of large birds. But she knew it would morph in the two hours (hour and forty-six minutes remaining) she had committed to staying.

"Andy!" cried Liz, a tall, gangly woman of about thirty, as she ran forward and wrapped her long arms around Andrea. Given her stature, Liz was probably the one who first suggested the image of geese. "I'm so glad you've come."

Liz's tone implied that she was surprised that Andrea had come, but pleasantly so. Andrea had always liked Liz, the way she immediately called her "Andy" and invited her into the office when she stopped by as if she were one of the team, stooping low to whisper information that could have been said aloud but seemed more exclusive and intimate when whispered.

"Let me introduce you around. You know Kate and this is . . ."

Andrea smiled and shook hands, trying to memorize the names but knowing it wouldn't matter in the end. This was just a pleasant respite where nothing was required of her until she could make it across the field to—what did the long table of books represent in this landscape? —the castle. Yes, the table was a fortress, with turrets of books.

"Have you read the book?" asked Kate. Her shiny, black hair was cut at a sharp angle, pointed and longer in the front, making Andrea think of a blade as it swung back and forth with her movements.

Before Andrea could answer, Liz cut her off. "Read it? Andy helped write it!"

"Not really," she said. "Ethan wrote everything. I just gave feedback."

"Ethan never mentioned that," said a redheaded woman, appropriately named Robin.

"He told me," said Liz. "And she's thanked in the acknowledgments."

"His *lawyer* is thanked in the acknowledgments," said Kate.

"*Boys!*" said Liz, and they all laughed. The instant camaraderie of women threw Andrea back to when she had first been initiated into the world of girls. With three older sisters, she should have been accustomed to it from an early age, but since she was six years younger than the next oldest, who were all a measured two years apart, she hadn't been invited in. She had only glimpsed their world through partially opened doors, overheard phone conversations, and by testing the piles of makeup they left around the rim of the bathroom sink. Most of her knowledge came from the clandestine world of slumber parties, parties that, in accordance with their moniker, blurred together in dreamlike memories, encampments of sleeping bags around a television or a fireplace. She remembered the slightly nauseated feeling one gets from eating too much junk food and staying up all night. The fuzzy seasickness the day after. One big blur. Only Ruby Randall's stood out.

~

Except for a wide space between her two front teeth that gave her a somewhat feral appearance, Ruby was a beautiful girl with pitch-black hair and eyes. She had been on the peripheral of their crowd in seventh grade, the height of slumber parties, mostly because she lived outside of town (the rest of them lived in town) in a small ranch house about three hundred feet from the tavern her parents owned. She had left their crowd entirely the following year when she elected the vocational training program in high school and the rest of them enrolled in college prep. But that summer, her backyard had been the site of the most notorious slumber party. It was the first time when "the boys" came and actually did more than peer in windows or slip in a back door, where they were told to shush lest they wake the parents. But at Ruby's house there were no parents to be seen. They must have been present for the drop-off, or who would have let their daughters stay? Maybe they had gone to the tavern? Andrea imagined there had been quite a few discussions among the parents, given the party was so far outside of town and so near a tavern with a borderline reputation. Andrea's mother wouldn't have cared. She was already exhausted from raising the older three girls, getting them safely off to college to think much about her. But the other parents might have objected if they had known the girls would be sleeping in the yard within full view of the tavern parking lot.

Seven or eight boys from their class hitchhiked out from town, bringing bottles of cheap wine and ziplock baggies of pot that was so mild it might have been oregano. The ones who had girlfriends at the party immediately disappeared into couples, under trees or into the bushes. It was a large backyard, much bigger than those in town, and since it was in the country, you could barely tell where the yard ended and a field of brambles that would later be sold and developed into a shopping mall began. The remaining boys found someone willing, leaving about four or five girls, including Andrea, around the firepit. They drank the wine—the first time Andrea had had more than a sip—and told stories until two grown men, wearing the ubiquitous uniform of boys her own age, flannel shirts and tattered jeans with ladders of white thread climbing the knee holes, came stumbling into the yard from the tavern. They might have been boys, if not for the fact that they were a bit beefier, a little more confident in their stride. A couple of the girls stood up shrieking, but then someone recognized the men. Robby and Mark Wilson were in their midtwenties. In their glory days, they had been part of a well-known local garage band. Their glory days were well behind them. They both worked in their father's hardware store, but still played an occasional gig, and they still carried a bit of their once legendary aura.

Robby squeezed in between Andrea and Jennifer Drake, looked at Jennifer, and then turned to Andrea. His eyes were glassy and his breath a mixture of sweet and sour that was strangely intoxicating.

"I'll show you how to drink wine," he said. He grabbed the bottle that was being passed around, tilted his head back, took a big swig, then held Andrea's face between his hands, leaned over, and kissed her, transferring the wine from his mouth into hers. She felt the sensation of the gush of sweet red wine followed by his tongue and imagined its large moist pinkness covered in taste buds. He turned more in her direction and continued kissing though the action was more like washing her mouth with his, creating a blurry, watery sensation that was surprisingly pleasant in the way it made her limbs feel loose and tingly. Though she had only a small amount of kissing experience, she easily fell in with the enterprise of their mouths moving in unison. She felt his hand creep up under her T-shirt and didn't stop it. She wanted to see how the fingers would feel on the growing mound beneath her bra. Who knows how far it would have gone if Mark hadn't pulled him away, saying: "Hey, Rob, we better get out of here. These are just kids."

The party was filled with events and pandemonium that ended in a screaming match between Ruby and her father, who wore a stained tank top. However, whenever Andrea recalled it, all the other events were dwarfed by the image of the taste-bud-speckled tongue and the memory of his rough fingertips on her smooth skin. And though she seldom saw Robby Wilson after that—and when she did, he didn't acknowledge her—the incident had cast her reputation as an adventuress.

The memory of Ruby's party triggered the memory of an essay Andrea had once tried to write on parties called "A Short History of Parties." She remembered looking up the word in both her Webster's and a dictionary of etymology. They had contradicted one another, the first saying that a party was a group coming together for amusement, while the latter said the word came from the Old French, "the past participle of *partie* divide." She had given up on the essay, always finding it to difficult to explain what she meant in nonfiction when fiction was available. But now when she looked around the room, she could see how a party both assembled and divided.

~

"You know he's quit, left Cromby's, don't you?" asked Liz.

"No, I didn't," said Andrea. Though not knowing was a tinge humiliating, she was not so foolish as to pretend she did know, thereby depriving herself of all the details. "When?"

Liz looked embarrassed, her cheeks flashing red.

"Just last week. He'll stay through the summer, but that's it." His job wasn't the kind where you could give two weeks' notice. There were too many costly projects.

"I knew he was thinking of opening a firm of his own."

"No," said Liz, leaning forward to whisper. "He's leaving to write. His contract was a two-book deal."

The news contained more of a blow than if she had been told he was leaving to join his secret polygamist family in Aruba. *She* was the writer. She had published three books, all with small presses, none of them getting the huge advance his had drawn. In fact, all of them together didn't amount to a fourth of his. But he never would have written the book if not for her. Unless they were out socially or in bed together, she had spent most of her time writing. She could revise a sentence a dozen times, searching for a perfection that only she would understand when she reached it.

Ethan had taken up writing to fill the time she wasn't available. Nor would he have come up with the frame for shaping it. True again, she couldn't have actually shaped the book like an architectural plan—he was the architect—but he wouldn't have thought of it if not for her. And all his characters would have remained flat if she hadn't pushed him. She had given over her whole life to writing, had forsaken marriage and family, even a real job. All through her twenties she had attended bridal showers and wedding receptions, feeling somewhat smug that her life would be different.

∼

"I guess you and Ethan will be next," Susan Butler had said to her at her bridal shower. They were standing in the archway of the dining room in Susan's mother's house, sipping from flutes of champagne, the stacks of silver-and-white packages spread out on the table like a distant snow-covered mountain range. Andrea and Ethan had been together for four years at the time.

"We're not planning on it."

"Really?" Susan had said. "Tell me the truth. I know you've always claimed you wanted this bohemian sort of life, dancing on tabletops, writing and taking on lovers and all that crap we used to say in college. But aren't you eventually going to want a family?"

"Maybe," she said, contradicting her word with an ironic smile. At the time, her second book had just come out and she was enjoying it almost as much as she had expected. She liked the contrasts of hard work and hard play. A time when it seemed she could drop a manuscript in the mail and her life could change when it reached an editor. Years later, she would enjoy the third book a little less so. And now the fourth manuscript, well, she was trying with agents and big houses for two years, but knew she would give up soon. The agents had all claimed to like the writing, but they needed more of a hook; nowadays publishers liked people who had done things other than write, had had things happen to them, writers with a *platform*. "I can't just make up a different life. The book is fiction, my life isn't," she had told one agent. He had responded with a question: "You sure you haven't had anything really tragic happen in your past that we could include in the bio, have you?"

∼

She had met Ethan at a party a few years after graduate school when she and Andy, the other Andy, the other "promising" one, were still hanging out together. "The two Andys," they were called, the girl-Andy and the boy-Andy. It had been one of those long nights, starting at a party in an upstairs flat in a huge, old Victorian house in Walker's Point that had been converted into apartments, moved to a bar, then another party in a cramped space decorated in Indian prints and slightly postcollege decor in the loft section of Milwaukee, where the boy-Andy met a tall, skinny guy wearing a white T-shirt, checked trousers, and bowler hat who was going to yet another party out in the suburbs. They piled in the back of someone's car—who knew how much the driver had had to drink—and took off, Andrea sitting on a stranger's lap in the back seat (boy-Andy was a buddy, not a lover).

As soon as they arrived and tumbled out of the car, Andrea knew it was a mistake. The house was huge, with four Corinthian columns in the front, undoubtedly someone's parents' house. The six or seven of them were all led by Bowler Head around back where the mistake became more evident. The guests stood clustered around the rear of the house, wearing shirt-waist flowered dresses, polo shirts, and khaki pants, sipping cocktails. *Not intended as ironic attire.* They were spaced as orderly as rows of freshly planted trees. Most of them were younger, still in college or grad school (law school, more likely) or just out. Instead of having a raucous party while their parents were away, they were practicing to become their parents. It must have been close to three in the morning at that point. How much practice did they need? They all still looked fresh. Were their drinks in their glasses practice as well? The host did not seem happy to see his bowler-hatted friend leading the motley crew.

"Let's go," Andrea whispered to Andy, tugging on his shirtsleeve. She knew her request was ridiculous. How could they leave? She didn't even know where they were, and they didn't have a car. Besides, boy-Andy was too blitzed to fully understand their circumstances. He didn't even hear her, having just noticed that the grassy yard swooped down to a long swimming pool, the water underlit in way that made it an unnatural mix of flickering liquid emerald and sapphire.

"Cool," he said and was off, stripping and discarding clothing as he made his way stumbling down the hill.

Andrea followed him, muttering, "Not a good idea, not a good idea."

He was naked by the time he got to the edge of the pool. Curling his toes over the edge, he spread his arms wide. His nakedness looked ghostly white in the pool lights. His penis, the only loose and jiggly protrusion on his otherwise flat and muscled body, looked particularly vulnerable. She was so glad she had never slept with him. A past sexual liaison would have made his present foolishness too sad to bear. At least his swan drive was magnificent. He followed it with a perfect full-length lap. She took off her shoes, rolled up her jeans, and waded her feet, waiting for his return. He swam the last few yards back to her underwater, a streak of pinkish flesh rippling beneath the brilliant blue-green surface. He popped up beside her dangling feet and shook the beads of water from his hair.

"Join me," he said.

"I don't think we should. No one else is."

"As soon as there are two of us, they'll come. You'll see," he said and pushed off from the side with his feet for another lap. Against her better judgment, Andrea slowly pulled her T-shirt over her head, unzipped her jeans, and slipped out of them and her panties without standing. Her bra was last before she lowered herself into the pool. Though she doubted it, she hoped Andy was right. Others joining in would be the only thing to save the situation. But regardless, she felt her only choice was to throw in her lot with Andy. She clung to the side, too embarrassed to swim and expose her bare behind to the crew at the top of the hill. As she had expected, there was no sound of huge movement, no rustle of shucking clothing. Only their bowler-hatted friend clapped and issued a little howl that sounded particularly plaintive in the surrounding silence. She looked up at the house. The rest of the guests seemed to be looking down their noses as if giant flies had landed in one of their giant martinis. She felt goose bumps forming. The pool wasn't heated and the cool pre-sunrise air was sweeping in from the west.

That was when Ethan appeared, trotting down the hill bearing an open purple towel. The scene, the landscape of the party, appeared to her like a battlefield where a momentary peace had been called.

"Looks like you need this," He said, offering her his hand and then wrapping her body in the towel the moment her feet were firm on the tile apron surrounding the pool.

"Can I give you a ride home?"

"I live all the way in downtown Milwaukee."

"Not a problem. I could use the drive."

"My friend . . ."

"He doesn't look quite ready to leave; besides, I'm sure he can go with Larry." Ethan was right; Andy did seem to be enjoying himself, splashing about. Larry—she assumed—was the guy in the bowler hat. He had arrived at the pool's edge and looked about ready to join Andy.

Andrea didn't remember getting dressed or walking through the crowd of onlookers. She did remember the ride into Milwaukee with Ethan chatting amicably as if they were on a date, telling her about his job at the architectural firm, about the advent of sustainable housing, how he had gone to the party at the insistence of his younger brother and was glad to have an excuse to leave. She wasn't quite sober, so both his words and his appearance confused her. He didn't see life as she did: hard work interrupted by frivolity. His thick eyelashes looked wet. He hadn't gone in the pool, had he? Later she would learn that his eyelashes looked perpetually wet, making clumps cling together so that his eyes resembled dark stars.

That pool party seemed to end the on-and-off-again series of drunken debacles she had experienced in college and grad school. Most of them were so formless in her mind that she wasn't even sure she could call them parties. Andrea didn't think they had had a role in shaping her the way the parties before or after higher education had. Rather, they left her groping for self-definition.

Andrea still had the towel from the evening. Lush purple, it was thicker after ten years than the towels she had freshly purchased; only the white monogram of "M" was beginning to lose thread, looking a bit plucked.

~

Andrea thought that the seemingly frivolous nature of the topic might have been another reason she had set aside the essay on parties. She wanted her readers to understand that a party could be more than a little event where people pretended to be brighter, happier, wittier, and more confident than they actually were. They were little microcosms of society, providing the only setting where she believed a person could arrive as one person and leave as another. But she could not find the words to convey the concept in exposition.

Andrea felt a warm hand cup her bare shoulder and turned to see Ethan.

"Glad you made it," he said.

"I said I would."

"I know, I know. It's just, well, I never would have written the book without you."

"I'm going to buy one . . . two."

"You don't have to do that. I'll write something in one and send it to you. I've been planning to."

"Great," she said. "Great. I was just about to come find you because I have to take off, but I wanted to come by and congratulate you."

"Already?" He looked at her with genuine kindness and affection. There really were people who weren't driven the way she was; people who didn't see the world as a series of dichotomies, landscapes to conquer or lose.

"Yeah, I've got another . . . thing to attend." She hadn't made it more than twenty-five minutes of her planned attendance, nor had she been able to come up with a better excuse than "a thing" for departing so early, but she found herself unable to last another minute. Oddly, her urge to leave didn't feel like failure. It seemed more like acceptance, an understanding that had taken a thousand parties to reach. She had felt there were two possibilities: either she would make it through the two hours with dignity, never revealing how she felt, or she would fail in a way where she would make a fool of herself, somehow exposing her desire and greed as she had at her sixth birthday party. Without trying, she had come to the realization that there was a third choice and it, to leave now, was the right one. The urgency in so much of what she had believed and felt during her life slipped away. She saw Will, sans sherbet-girl, weaving his way through the room toward them. Maybe he had thought of an answer to her question regarding something he had recently finished that initially seemed too difficult? Or maybe he had some other thought he wanted to share. It didn't matter. She placed what remained of her beer under a light on the bar so that the inch of amber liquid glowed. The freedom of the moment was so profound and so clear that she was afraid it couldn't last, but she had to take the risk that it would by kissing Ethan on the cheek and walking out of the room before the space transformed itself.

Wheels

Ace Rivers leaned into the wind as he walked. He knew if he stood up straight, he would be blown backward, his arms flailing wildly like a broken windmill until he either steadied himself or fell hard on his behind. It would hurt; he knew it would hurt. All of his bones hurt these days—even without a fall—as if they were on fire from within. He imagined the pain would be intense with only his khaki pants separating his tailbone from the concrete. Yet that was not the part that bothered him. It was the embarrassment. People running from every direction to help him up, to assist the frail old man, all of them talking loudly with exaggerated enunciation, assuming his hearing diminished or—worse—his mind.

At the moment, pitching forward, weaving between dozens on the crowded sidewalk, he felt invisible, the way old men are among the young and the firm. If he fell, he would appear in full color, the poor, old man, a heap of bones and fabric, maybe a trickle of blood running from an ancient orifice. He knew that everyone under forty-five viewed being old as a permanent state, perhaps bad luck, perhaps a reflection of character. Intellectually they knew that they too would age, but in practice, they thought people came into this world old or young. If people actually became old it was a result of bad behavior, something the old person had brought upon themself; perhaps by not exercising enough, not eating organic foods, or not drinking enough mineral water. None of them could look at his birdlike bones and believe he had once been young, like them, *younger even*, an athlete, a bicyclist.

Ace turned on Wabash and headed south. A teenager on a skateboard swerved around him—*swishhhhh*—in a graceful S. A woman yelled, "Off the sidewalk!" Ace agreed. The kid should not be on the sidewalk; still, Ace liked the roaring sound of the wheels as well as the elegance of the kid's maneuver. Ace turned slightly to watch the teenager, skinny and white with dyed-black hair, like a movie chimney sweep, disappear behind him into the wall of people.

Ace had always liked wheels. From the time he was a toddler and given his first toy dump truck, he had loved watching them spin, loved any vehicle that traveled by things beneath it going round and round and round. He could still recollect the taciturn feel of shoving his miniature trucks and cars through the dirt that bordered his backyard and alley, creating roads in the grime. He knew the names of all the trucks—tow, garbage, dump, flatbed—before he could pee straight into a toilet. He had received his first bicycle in 1936, when he was five years old. A red Ranger Ace. He had never seen anything so beautiful. He had learned to ride it in one day. The bike was where he earned his nickname. That night when he had returned at sunset, his knees and elbows scrapped and stinging from multiple falls— falls that felt *good*, proof of his triumphs—his father had looked up from the evening paper (*evening*, they had a morning and an evening then) and said, "Well, if it isn't Ace!" The nickname had stuck. He became a bicycle messenger in Chicago before the war—*swissshhhh*, cutting through the air, *flying*, up on curbs, down into gutters, between cars, flying, flying, flying.

He had been flying ever since he was five, anything on wheels, a bike in the city, a jeep in the army, and a series of cars—until last week when his children had taken away his keys.

His children. His car. His keys.

How was that possible? He stood still and braced himself against a sudden gust. These side streets that ran east and west off Michigan Avenue were murder, like wind tunnels. He waited until the gust had passed and resumed his walk, still springy by any standards.

It had been a surprise, their offer to bring over pizza for dinner two Sundays ago. Usually one of them visited, once a week. He imagined they had worked it out, taking turns. He should have guessed something was up. *Both on the same night when it wasn't his birthday or a holiday?*

His two children had returned to Chicago after college. Well, actually, Jeff had never left. He had lived at home during college, gotten a job at the *Trib*, been laid off, tried his hand at novels—no good apparently with the imagination—and gone to freelancing and writing a *blog*. Ace couldn't think of the word without remembering the movie, *The Blob*, a mess of a monster. Ace had taken Jeff to see it when he was what—eight? Ten? Jeff had covered his eyes and curled into the back of his theater seat, a terrified coil. Ace could still picture the bend of his little boy spine in the red-and-blue-striped T-shirt. Lucky Jeff had never married. Who could support a family on the peanuts he must be earning on that silly blog? Ace's daughter,

Penny, was a hospital administrator, had two great kids, but his grandkids were teenagers now. He hardly saw them.

A few days after their Sunday visit, Ace had looked up Jeff's blog—Jeff probably figured Ace was either too senile to remember he wrote a blog or figured him not capable of locating it. The title of his most recent entry was more or less what Ace would have expected:

When Is It Time to Take Away Your Parents' Car Keys?

Despite the fact he was expecting some such foolery, he was seized with rage at the words. The end of his dignity, fodder for Jeff's *blob*. What was the point of Jeff's blog anyways? An advice column? Ace remembered when Jeff was little how carefully Marianne had followed all the advice in Dr. Spock's baby-and-child guide, like it was some sort of Bible or Bill of Rights.

Maybe that's how Jeff would make his mark. Become the baby boomers' version of Spock, giving advice to middle-aged and older children about how to care for their aging parents. *When Is It Time to Reverse Potty Training, Put Your Folks Back in Diapers? How Do You Know When Your Parents Need to Be Sent to a Home? What to Do When Your Parents Can No Longer Handle Their Finances.* Ace thought of how his old friend Hank would laugh at these thoughts. Hank was one of the few people who understood Ace's humor perfectly. Ace laughed aloud and started to cough, that deep, dry hacking cough he had had off and on for the last few years. He stopped walking, stood still, clung to a streetlamp pole, and waited for the cough to pass. Walking, coughing, and wind didn't mix. He coughed so hard that a bit of pee squeezed from the tip of his penis. *Shit.* He didn't think it was more than a drop, not enough to go beyond his boxers and appear on his outer pants. *Boxers.* He remembered how Jeff had worn briefs, laughed at his father's "old-man" boxers. Now both Penny's boys wore boxers. They called Jeff's briefs "tighty-whities." Ace smiled. What goes around comes around. He was sorry he wouldn't be around to see those boys take away Penny's keys. But who would take Jeff's?

Ace was sobered by the memory that Hank was dead, had died six months ago. He hadn't forgotten really, but given he had known Hank for over sixty years, it was not easy to dismiss the idea of telling him things. Over the last few years, so many friends had died that he sometimes had a hard time remembering who was still kicking and who wasn't, but he was surprised to find he had temporarily forgotten in which world Hank resided. The thought sobered Ace. He stopped coughing and continued walking.

They had been sitting at his kitchen table, eating the pizza, when Jeff broached the subject.

"Dad, there is something Penny and I need to talk to you about."

Penny cut her pizza slice with a knife and fork. It was plain cheese. No onions or pepperoni, the way he liked. *Bad for your stomach*, Penny had said. *Acid reflux. That's one of the reasons you can't stop coughing.* Pizza didn't look as tasty when cut into bite-sized pieces.

"Well, I'm here. Talk," said Ace.

"This is hard, Dad," said Jeff. As he watched his son's lips move, Ace tried to remember why they had named him Jeff. It wasn't a family name, just popular at the time. Marianne had liked the sound of it. *Modern*, she said. Jeff had had a lot of hair at birth. Penny had had none. It was strange how those things worked; Marianne had bobby-pinned a bow to Penny's one tuft. They had cut Jeff's when he was less than a month old. "But, well, Dad, we think it is time that, maybe, well, you stopped driving."

The words didn't register at first. What were they talking about? He wasn't driving. He was sitting there at the table, eating pizza. Pretty bland pizza, at that.

"Time to hang up the keys, Dad," said Penny. "We mean after the accident and all."

Burning rage shot from his chest to his brain, like his head could pop off. He could barely sputter a response.

"What are you talking about? *That accident was nothing. It was their fault, the way they positioned the signs.*"

"You did get a ticket."

"The cops have their quotas."

"Dad, *you drove up onto the sidewalk*, almost into the store window. If anyone had been walking past, you might have killed them."

"*Well*," he spit out the word. "*No one was walking, were they?*" Ace didn't like how cranky he sounded, how defensive. He wouldn't maintain the upper hand if he lost his cool.

"And what about the one-way street by my house? You were parked the wrong way almost two feet from the curb all day on Thanksgiving."

"Anyone could make the mistake. All those one-ways out by you."

"And the Hamilton boy's tricycle?"

"He left it in my drive . . . and I paid for a new one!"

The conversation continued for nearly an hour. Penny talking about Peapod and home delivery services. All the "research" they had done. Ace snickered at how typing a question into Google constituted as research these days. He felt he mounted a good defense, had even calmed down until Jeff suggested an adult tricycle.

"Just for neighborhood errands—you won't be able to ride it into the Loop or anything."

Ace burst from his chair and hurled his half-eaten third slice at the wall. The cheese and sauce stuck, but the remainder of the triangular crust did a backflip onto the floor.

"*A fucking tricycle?*" He had never used the f-word in front of his children. In fact, he seldom used it at all. He knew that was a bit prudish, given the times. But except in the war, no one used the word in his day. If Marianne were alive, they probably wouldn't even have his subscription to cable, given the word's omnipresence in movies and the series on HBO and Showtime.

An image of himself and Hank, two oldsters, racing down Racine on giant tricycles flashed across his mind and he laughed out loud. *LOL*, he had learned from his youngest grandson. LOL. He laughed at the idea of the acronym. Laughing and coughing. Laughing the way he did must have made him look crazy to his children. He tried to stop, which exacerbated his coughing. LCOL. He became so stooped from hacking that he couldn't speak.

"Dad, are you all right?" asked Penny, twisting her waist, leaning down from her chair to look up into what must have been his scarlet face.

He pointed at his root beer and she handed it to him. After a few sips, he felt composed. He sat back in his chair.

"I think this discussion has come to an end," said Ace. "I have listened to what you've had to say, and I think we will just need to agree to disagree. After all, I am a licensed driver and there is nothing you can do."

No one spoke for over a minute.

"Well, Dad, I was hoping it wouldn't get to this," said Jeff. "But actually there is something we can do."

Ace looked at Penny and Jeff. *His children.* He had pushed Jeff along on his bike after the training wheels had been removed. Ace had not sat in his armchair and smoked and read the paper like his own father had done. No, Ace had been out there in the street with Jeff an entire Saturday. He remembered Marianne drawing a red snake of Mercurochrome on the one and only scrape Jeff had on his knee. Mercurochrome had mercury in it, Ace remembered. The government must have banned it at some point, like they did getting your feet x-rayed when you bought a pair of shoes. Ace had liked that, seeing the bones of his feet. Ace couldn't remember how Penny had learned to ride. Surely, she had ridden a bike, hadn't she? Had Marianne taught her?

For what must have been a full two minutes, no one blinked. Ace did not want to hear from his children what the "something" they could do was; he would rather concede than learn what more their "research" had revealed.

"Well, okay," he said. "I guess you win; I won't drive. I'll just leave the keys right there on the hook by the door."

All three pairs of their eyes shifted to the keys, a clump hanging from the upturned trunk of a little wooden elephant hook that one of his grandsons had given him a dozen birthdays ago. Again, no one spoke. *They weren't actually planning to take his keys, were they?*

"Dad," Penny cupped her right hand over his hand and drew her eyebrows together in concern. She looked like Marianne, except not as pretty, a washed-out version of Marianne. Marianne had prided herself on her natural curls. Penny straightened her hair to hang limp. Ace noticed Penny's hand had a few liver spots, a popping vein, but nothing compared to the gnarled, bony mess of his hand. He pulled his hand out from under hers, a gentle tug. He didn't want her to think this was a lovey-dovey, father/daughter moment. "We will leave you the keys—in case of an emergency, and I do mean a *real* emergency—but we *are* going to check the mileage and, well, if it goes up . . ."

She shrugged. Jeff finished for her.

"We will have to take the car."

Ace stared at them. Who were these people and how had they gained such control over his life? Were they really his family? Could he just empty his savings and drive down to Florida and never contact them again? Would they find him through his social security or his pension? He remembered when Jeff, a senior in high school, had taken his car—without asking—and gone to that concert in Wisconsin. Didn't return until the next day. He should have reported it stolen, had Jeff locked up, instead of simply grounding him. Why had he paid for their college educations? Helped Penny and her husband buy their first house? None of it was clear now.

"Dad, you have to understand how hard this is for us," said Jeff.

That was a point Ace would later see that Jeff emphasized in his blog. How hard it was for *him*. Jeff didn't seem to grasp what it might be for Ace. No wonder he hadn't made it as a novelist, no empathy for his subject.

Jeff had come the following Sunday to check Ace's mileage and take him out for a bite. Penny and her husband, Craig, came the next week. When Craig said, "Hi, Ace," Ace had said "Call me Roger now; the name on my birth certificate." Ace couldn't remember if he had told his children how he got his nickname—had they ever bothered to ask?

Ace had kept his word; he hadn't driven. He didn't want to rush into anything unplanned. If he did take off, he might have to abandon the house and most of the contents. Unless he was prepared to drive to Florida and never look back, he knew they had him. He wasn't sure it mattered. Most of the objects had belonged to Marianne—the furniture, the paintings, the knickknacky stuff. He only cared about it because the stuff reminded him of Marianne. She had an eye for things, what would look nice on a shelf, what was too much clutter. Hank had always envied him that, how Marianne could keep a house. Hank's wife, Leslie, had never been one for domestic skills. An anthropologist—they called her a "lady" anthropologist back in the day—but she sure was prettier than that famous lady anthropologist, Margaret Mead. Leslie, a professor, usually had her nose in a book or was off on a field trip or something. But, boy, when she put all that stuff aside, the four of them had a gas! The parties they had had!

One Halloween, both Marianne and Leslie had dressed as flappers. Leslie found a dress in a used clothing store and Marianne actually had one that her mother had worn. They both wore feathers in their hair and long necklaces. They were young mothers by then but had perfect girlish figures. As a joke, Leslie had filled her and Hank's old claw-footed bathtub with gin and pink lemonade. Everyone drank from it with punch cups. At some point, the gals had done the Charleston on Leslie's kitchen counter. The kitchen was packed with people, everyone cheering them on. What a night! Penny and Jeff had been asleep in one of the upstairs bedrooms. Around three in the morning, he and Marianne—drunk as skunks—had staggered up to get them and carried them both to the car. They took Ashland Avenue—flying through at least one red light—from Evanston where Hank and Leslie lived to the little house in West Rogers Park where he and Marianne lived, where he *still* lived. The next morning, Ace couldn't remember the drive back into the city. Jeff might have had a point if he had taken away the keys *that* night. But Jeff was only about four years old, he and Penny asleep in the back seat—no seat belts, of course—and no clue that his dad was snookered.

~

Ace ducked into a doorway, away from the wind. He felt like he had gone too far south. According to his calculations he should have been there by now. He pulled the crumpled map from his pocket. He had written down the directions himself because he didn't believe online maps were accurate. After his years as a messenger, he knew the city better than any Internet mapmaker. Of course, who could tell anything now with the way things had changed? All the old landmarks gone. Imagine, a Target in the old Louis Sullivan building! Ace looked at where he had marked an X for SuperDuper Car Rental, the cheapest deal he could find. Yes, it seemed he had walked far enough from the El. He would try one more block then turn around. He stepped back into the wind.

Before he left town, he would visit Leslie at that place. She wouldn't know him. During Hank's last year alive, she had not even known Hank. But she would provide a familiar face for Ace to tell his plans. She would be friendly and pretend to know him. *Oh, it's you!* she would say cheerfully. Hank's oldest son, Rick, had taken over the socket-making business Ace and Hank had started after college. The plan had been for Rick and Jeff to run it together, but Jeff had wanted no part of it, so Ace and Hank had worked out a complicated plan where most of his share was sold to Rick. Ace remained a primary stockholder, but not enough to keep Rick from moving operations down south for lower wages, a plan Rick came up with only a month after Hank died. Ace was glad that Hank wouldn't be around to see the old building go dark, the men laid off. He and Hank had always gotten on well with the union. A lot of the guys had even come to their parties, mixed well with the colleagues Leslie invited from her department at Loyola. He wondered if Rick had found a place for Leslie in South Carolina or if he was just going to leave his mother behind. Ace was glad that Marianne had died without him having to make the sort of decision that Hank had faced with Leslie. Ace supported Hank's choice. How was Hank supposed to keep changing her diapers, washing her hair, dressing her, and fixing all the meals when his own hands were, like Ace's, gnarled from arthritis? On top of that, he was having a difficult time controlling his blood pressure. Sure, Hank had had that Filipino woman in the daytime—but he didn't want her there 24-7, spending the night every night. When Marianne had died so many years earlier—only sixty-eight years old—it had seemed a tragedy! Now, it seemed a bit of a blessing that she never had to face the indignities of the elderly, only the minor inconveniences of the old. With the cancer, she went quickly.

At least by disappearing, Ace wouldn't need to stomach the talk where Penny and Jeff informed him that they were putting him in a home or read on Jeff's blog—*How to Dump Dad?* Ace assumed that post was next.

Ace had a lot to accomplish before he took off. Planning would take at least two more weeks, and he needed a car. Except for starting his car once a day to keep the battery in shape, he wasn't going anyplace in it until he had every detail of the plan in order. All he knew for sure was that his departure would be on a Monday morning, the day after one of his off-spring had come to check mileage. He wanted a full week for his getaway. On the drive down south, he thought he might swing by the place Rick had purchased for the company's new location. He wouldn't be able to stop in. By the time he reached South Carolina, Penny or Jeff might have called Rick, alerted him to the fact that they had an escaped father on their hands. But Ace could drive by. Thankfully Penny had made him buy that stupid cell phone, and they rarely called him on the landline—in fact, they usually only called once a week. Okay, he had to admit, Penny sometimes called more. He had to give her credit for that.

Ace hoped he could wrangle a dinner with his grandsons before he left. He had a couple items he wanted to give them. If not, he imagined he could leave the things in his house with their names taped to the items. He knew he would never be able to contact them again. Would they all think he had done himself in? Ace cast the thought aside; to get mushy or senti-mental could cause the whole plan to crumble.

His prescriptions were a problem. He took eight pills a day, fewer than some his age. He wondered if he could simply have his doc switch them when he settled in Florida. Was Dr. Graham obligated to tell his children Ace's location or did the HIPAA laws protect him regardless of age? Ace thought he might be safe in Florida, blend in with the other sun birds; they had so many laws to protect seniors down there. He doubted they had extradition laws to Illinois. Ha. Ha. He started laughing again. LCOL. Hank would get a chuckle out of that one. Whenever they had a major situation at work—an order running behind, a cash-flow problem—one of them would step into the other's office, arch an eyebrow, and say, *Ready to skip to Mexico?* It was just too bad Ace couldn't leave his worn-out body behind in Illinois.

Ace paused to clear his throat, glanced across the street. Miller's Pub. He and Hank had loved that place, so had Freddie, head of the union. Maybe he would have a beer and a burger before he got the car. A celebration of sorts.

Wait! He felt his whole body spring to attention.

What was Miller's Pub doing across the street? If he was heading south, Miller's Pub wouldn't be anyplace nearby at all. *Had he been walking north? How was that possible?* Back in his bike messenger days, he liked to say that a person couldn't get lost in the Loop, given the grid and the lake. But there was only one explanation for Miller's Pub being across the street. He must have walked north from the El station. *Really?* He shook his head, trying to shake off his sudden disorientation. He had simply been distracted; who wouldn't be with what his kids were putting him through!

He spun around quickly veering to the right and—Swishhhh! *Wham!* A sharp, pointed object—an axe? No, an elbow? —stabbed his chest. Ace saw he had collided with the boy, the tall, skinny boy, the chimney sweep on the skateboard. Midair, Ace arched his back, hoping to prevent his tailbone from cracking against the sidewalk; a mistake, he realized, as the crown of his skull struck the concrete. He closed his eyes, then opened them again. *See,* Ace thought, *the boy had changed directions too. Anyone can go the wrong way. Even a young teenager.* The boy was holding the board, its wheels still spinning. *Wow, that kid had a sharp elbow. Is this it?* he thought. *Is this how he would die? Was it too late to disinherit his children? Rock, paper, scissors.* He sat up and fell back again. A kaleidoscope of color and abstract images spun above him; hanging ties, one striped, one yellow against a blue lapel, the red shoulder of a woman's blouse, dangling hair and concerned eyes, and denim, a forest of denim posts. *Did he break something? He felt sick. Marianne was going to kill him. She wanted him to quit the bike job before they graduated, before the wedding. But he needed the money for his share of the business. Who was that crying boy? Did he know him? It seemed like he did. Dressed in black with very black hair, the boy was white as a corpse. The boy was sobbing, his bony winglike shoulders heaving up and down.*

"Stand back."

Did he say that or was it someone else? Not his voice.

"Is he conscious?" It was a man talking. He seemed to have a tiny walkie-talkie in his hand.

Yes, of course, he answered, without moving his lips. He had fallen from his bike a hundred times, a thousand, maybe. Never broken a bone.

"His eyes were open a second ago; now they're closed! Did you call 911?"

And, then, in what seemed like seconds, Marianne was there. Had the man reached her by walkie-talkie? Thankfully, Marianne did not seem at all angry. She helped him up and into the car. How had she found a parking spot on Wabash? And where did she get this car? Blue with white-leather seats. He had always wanted a convertible. Maybe he had bought it and forgotten. Such an extravagance. He hoped he hadn't used any of the money he and Hank had set aside for the business. Maybe it was a surprise, a wedding gift. From his father—that explained why his dad hadn't sprung much for college, he wanted to give Ace a car. It didn't matter where it came from; nothing mattered as long as Marianne wasn't angry with him, as long as they could continue like this, him at the wheel, with Marianne scooted right next to him, her head on his shoulder, her curly hair tickling his right cheek. His left hand gripped the wheel while his right arm draped her shoulder. He loved the feel of the wind and the sound of the spinning tires. It had been a long time since he had been this happy. He felt the wide grin spread his cheeks as they sailed up Lake Shore Drive, with the sparkling water of Lake Michigan—cerulean, with cottony white caps—spread out endlessly to their right, like a roiling, liquid heaven.

Breaking News

I stand, my thumb poised to hit the off button, when *Breaking News* flashes across the screen. I am always a sucker for this. No matter how many times "breaking" means a follow-up to news that broke four days ago, or the "news" is actually a reality star's divorce, I keep thinking something important might have happened. So I withdraw my thumb. And then, there *you* are, on the screen. I sink back on the ottoman, with the channel turner—directed at the television—clutched in my hand, as if rigor mortis has set in. I pull the ottoman even closer to the screen.

I immediately see him in your eyes. Even if your last name had not been on the bottom of the screen (how many people have the surname MacGiolla?), I think I would have recognized you in him. You have the same squint—as if staring into bright light—giving way to sparkling iced-tea colored irises. Of course, the color on my television screen doesn't fully capture your distinct shade of yellow-brown, but I know it so well: topaz peeking out from that perpetual squint. Yet it seems impossible. It's as if I dug up a time capsule in the backyard that I had actually planted in an imaginary country.

You look serious, as well you should given the circumstances. You are in one of those cities where bombs go off in the metro or the mall or the airport. Of course, those are all cities now. New York. Paris. Brussels.

This time, Berlin.

Five minutes until we need to leave!

I hear my husband calling, but I am frozen in place, watching you.

Your cheeks are pink. A gold scarf is coiled around your neck, to bring out your eyes no doubt. Perhaps you consider them your finest feature. People have probably told you, again and again, *you have your father's eyes,* but I imagine you have long since stopped thinking of them as his. He is a man and you are a beautiful girl—sorry, woman now—so who would care more about his eyes than yours?

You need to understand, all things are temporary. Those eyes will remain yours no longer than they were his.

You grasp the stem of your microphone as if a blast might blow it from your grip. It is a distinct possibility. Smoke still lingers in the air behind you. People are scurrying. Sirens wail.

I knew you planned to be a journalist, though I didn't know you had actually become one, or that you had become an international correspondent. Your father and I lost touch after the night they arrested Sonny so long ago, and, then, didn't see each other again until fifteen years ago. What a funny expression, *lost touch*. As if we were the figures on the Sistine Chapel, our fingers barely brushing one another before a bolt of lightning sends a connection charging through us. The last time I saw your father before our meeting fifteen years ago, we sat facing each other on that long, ratty green sofa we had pulled from the alley, the springs gone, the cushions so sunk that it was more like we were sitting in a boat together. Our arms up, our palms planted against each others,' as if on opposite sides of plate glass.

"You can come with me," he said. "Please, I want you to come."

"I can't," I said.

"You won't," he said. I know those weren't the last words we spoke, but they are the last I remember him saying that night, him thinking I wouldn't go when in fact I couldn't.

And then, there you are, his daughter, in my living room, standing in front of rubble in a terrorist-rocked place, and your father's words echo.

You won't.

I wonder if you know anything about me. It seems unlikely. No, no, of course not; parents never tell their children those stories. *The stories that really make up a life.*

Even if you and I met, I could not convey our relationship to you, the confident woman with the microphone. *So, you knew my father in college,* you might say. Or, even, *You dated, hmmm, interesting.* Dated! Such a concept. As if *dating* even existed during that era; your father, wearing a letter sweater, pulling up to the curb to get me in a red convertible. Ha! That was not the world we lived in then. I doubt I could ever explain to you, a face on television, how deeply we—you and I—are linked. I knew your grandmother who died before you were born. I am the one who clutched your father's waist as he sped around campus on his motorcycle. I am the one who took care of your father after his wisdom teeth were extracted. I am the only person he ever told about the boy he bullied in grade school. I never saw your father so anguished as when he admitted to how he had tortured that boy. I think his guilt was partly what radicalized him, against the war, yes, but also against all injustices.

I know these things you will never know.

If at some point you decide to swab the interior of your cheek, explore your genealogy, you will not find my ancestors. It's possible your father might not even recognize me if he saw me today. After a few started and failed careers, I am now a museum curator at a small but well-endowed decorative arts museum, and on the distant side of middle age, not what most people would consider extraordinary. But I exist in your father's DNA, deep in the tissues of his brain, perhaps his heart. He in mine.

We met when I worked at the Student Center, taking photos of students for their ID cards. They each stood on an X of yellow tape adhered on the floor in front of a white wall. I got them in my sights and clicked. Afterward, I placed the photo beside a card with the university logo and the student's name in a little plastic pouch, then inserted the pouch on a carrier and fed it through the laminating machine. During the last step of the process, I fit the sealed card in a frame on a trimming machine and pulled a heavy lever to trim the edges. The process was vaguely satisfying—except during the first week of the semester, when one card immediately followed another, a line out the door of the small, windowless office. My coworker and I stood behind the counter maneuvering large, black cameras on poles, constantly snapping, feeding, and cutting, my arm growing sore from yanking the lever.

Your father came into the office during the third or fourth week, the minute my partner walked out on her lunch break. I guess he was waiting to catch one of us alone. It was mere chance that it turned out to be me.

"I need a new ID," he said. Silky blond hair fell to his shoulders, and those lethal golden eyes. Handsome but in an unconventional way. When he smiled I saw his front teeth grew behind his incisors which gave him a feral—wolfish—appearance, almost as if he had fangs.

"I need your driver's license or a birth certificate," I said. "And your registration slip."

"Don't have either," he responded, and smiled broadly, his wolfish grin. He took a step backward, onto the yellow X, so that he stood in my line of vision; then, he dramatically pulled out the lining of his empty blue jeans pockets to demonstrate how bereft he was of documentation.

"Then how can I make you an ID?" I asked, cocking my head and turning my lips up in what I hoped was a provocative smile. With most kids, I would have instructed them to return when they had all their documents, but we were the only two in the office and he was so striking. I look at young men now, men in their early twenties, and wonder if the first time I saw him, your father looked as young as they do. I wonder if the young men of today—who all look the same to me—would be more distinguishable and interesting if I were their age.

"With that camera, based on my good word," he said. He walked up to fold his arms on the counter. He wore a fatigue jacket. He lowered his head to place his chin on top of his folded arms and looked up at me, playfully beseeching.

Have you seen my keys?

Look on the kitchen counter.

I am surprised by the sound of my voice responding to my husband, surprised that I can speak.

To this day, I don't know why I did it. I was a good girl, the same way I am a good woman today. Above average in all things—but not far above in any one thing. I think I wanted that one thing that would allow me to be exceptional. Breaking a rule impulsively, at that moment, seemed to be that one thing. The next week, when he returned, again on my partner's lunch break, and asked for another ID with another name, I again complied.

"So, did your name change?" I asked as I inserted the pouch in the laminating machine.

"No, same name as last week, but I have a new identity, so I had to find a new name."

We both laughed, and while I finished processing his card, he invited me to meet him at the anti-war rally the next day. Did you, lady on the television, know that he organized demonstrations? As with everyone else I knew, I was opposed to the war, but not with his passion, not to the point of organizing groups.

Before long, we were lovers and I was making IDs for friends he brought in at lunch time, students and nonstudents. First Sonny, who anyone would describe as a gentle bear. Standing at six feet and well over two hundred pounds with a fuzzy, brown beard, he invited the cliché. Gentle giant. He was even more distant from the university than your father, who had at least attended. Sonny was a high school dropout, a former foster child, who needed the ID to get into school assemblies. Some of the others used the fake IDs to get illegal drivers' licenses, others to log into buildings under false names. I never knew all their reasons, but I would have done anything for your father.

Are young women still like that today? Girls used to do crazy things for boys. I can't say there wasn't a part of me that didn't like the idea of doing something daring and rebellious, but in my heart I know I did it primarily for him.

Distributing fake IDs aside, we behaved like most of the other students of our era, but I believe we were more, that we did not invite the cliché of our times the way Sonny attracted the bear comparison. We were lovers who talked of action, your father and I, lovers who talked of peace and possibilities. Most nights we spent in your father's room, over the soup kitchen, on the damp mattress planted on the floor, our young bodies molding our shapes into the striped ticking. Three pulsating lava lights providing the only eerie illumination in the room. Psychedelic band posters plastered the walls, along with one of Chairman Mao in his green worker's uniform buttoned at the throat. Maybe we were more of a cliché than I like to believe? Certainly his decor was standard issue of the day. Before or after or in between lovemaking, we solved the world's problems, over and over. He would pluck a text from his leaning bookcase—made of bricks supporting boards—the requisite *The Communist Manifesto*, *The Autobiography of Malcolm X*, or the Little Red Book, and read to me. When he leaned on an elbow to explain his vision, his squinting eyes seemed to see beyond me to a future utopia only we understood, as if he held his sparkling apparition between the lids of his eyes. The term *love nest* was made for that room. The only other furniture was the broken green couch and a wobbly card table. The smell of weed, patchouli, and of sex—sex as raw as it would ever be, propelled by his lizard hips and smoothly muscled arms. Clothes scattered around the mattress. At some point, I moved out of my dorm room and joined him in not attending classes, yet I thought I knew where we were going. I felt more driven by our activities than I ever had by my studies. We clung to each other every night as we slept, were still clinging when we awoke in the morning.

Yet I was taken by surprise when your father told me of the plan to rob the bank truck.

"An armed truck?" I laughed.

I knew he was serious when he didn't laugh back. The lava lamps seemed to go wild, thumping up and down, casting purple and green shadows on his skin as he leaned over me, tracing my lips with his right index finger, partly to quiet me, partly to arouse me.

"We need the money to finance our operation. And we need you to be a decoy. I didn't want it to be you, but we need someone we trust."

I grabbed his finger with my teeth, and then shook it loose.

"What are you talking about? We don't need much money for the rallies."

"No, no, no, not those. Talk isn't cutting it anymore. I'm sorry, really, I am, to ask you this, but your part is small. All you need to do is walk up to the truck at their second stop, as they open the back doors—that branch doesn't have its own guard—ask the bank truck guard for directions, we'll be hiding across the street."

I never did learn all the details of the plan or the date—*safer that way*, your father said (sounds like a bad movie script when I recall it now), only that I was supposed to wear my red paisley miniskirt and scoop-necked leotard top. A part of me didn't like the idea; I tried to talk him out of it, woo your father away from drastic measures, offer alternatives. Peaceful things we could do for peace, rather than war on war. No use. By then, his anger had grown too fierce. I never would have gone even as far as discussing violence if not for him, if not for his beautiful eyes, my love for him, for his vision. His eyes. *Your eyes.*

In the end, I was not tested. A bank teller, the girlfriend of one of the other boys, was caught making photocopies of the truck route. She gave up her boyfriend, who was arrested. Your father and I watched him on the news, his scruffy beard and downcast eyes, being taken from his apartment along with Sonny, his T-shirt riding up his large belly, revealing soft flesh. Both Sonny's and the other guy's arms were pulled behind them, locked in handcuffs. I remember feeling bad that Sonny couldn't free his hands to pull his shirt down. I don't remember if news stories were announced back then with the flashing words—*Breaking News*—but I do recall how the news *broke us* when the reporter, with the Farrah Fawcett hairstyle, said the police were seeking additional suspects.

"You won't," your father said later that night, dropping his hands from mine, the light leaving his eyes. I couldn't be on the run, not then.

I wanted to tell him why I couldn't, about his child growing inside of me. But how could I complicate his getaway with such information? Instead I didn't tell him and he left in a huff.

Sophie Berg, a girl with frizzy, brown hair spreading from both sides of her central part like a long skirt, took me for the abortion, a doctor's office after hours. Four hundred fifty dollars. A lot of money then, but a huge risk for the doctor. Another fifty dollars for an anesthetic; we didn't know, we didn't have the money, so no anesthetic. Instead Sophie held my hand and stroked my brow. I barely knew her, but she was a friend of your father's, the only one who knew how to find a willing doctor. I remember her hands were calloused. I wanted them to be soft.

Can anyone who has not felt it imagine what it feels like for your insides to be scraped, a sharp spoon licking a soft bowl? No wonder I bucked, causing the little tear that would lead to a big tear, to my insides coming undone. Sophie took me back to your father's, where I bled, soaking the mattress, holding my knees tightly together, trying to staunch the flow, quell the cramps. A week later, after the ER, after the surgery, after returning to the room over the soup kitchen, I clutched my stomach, felt I was holding what was left of my insides together, as I dragged the drenched and crusty mattress down the stairs to the back alley. I looked at the spot where I had tried to press my legs together, a deep black-red starburst, still moist, like old jam, in the center.

I thought your father was gone for good, in that strange country of the past with all the buried time capsules. If not for the Internet, he would have been. We would not have been able to meet for coffee in Boston fifteen years ago, sit at that little wobbly table on the sidewalk, and nostalgically recall the wobbly card table in the apartment over the soup kitchen. I would not have listened to him tell me of you or of his wife, *your mother*, a woman who put him up in the makeshift underground when he was on the run, a woman who was willing to go with him when he traveled to the next place on the list.

"She went with me," he said, and we both knew he meant *you wouldn't*. He wore a gold tie that brought out his eyes.

You won't.

I was kind enough not to remind him of the fact that he never really had to go on the run. No one was looking for him. He was never an actual outlaw. Even the charges against Sonny had been dropped. Still, as the head of a nonprofit for inner city youth, he had continued to walk the walk. I didn't want to dismiss his commitment. What I could have told him, wanted to tell him, was why I didn't go. But what was the point after so many years? Instead I told him about my career and implied I had chosen not to have children because of it.

He said, not unkindly, "I guess you weren't the stand-by-your-man type." I think he intended to break the tension; instead the words intensified it.

If not for the Internet, if not for so many things—if not for the woman making college IDs with me going to lunch first, if not for the bank teller giving the plan up before we enacted it, if not for Sonny keeping his lips sealed, if not for the birth that never happened—I might not be sitting here now in a color-coordinated gray, white, and black Eileen Fischer ensemble, waiting for my husband to locate his keys so we can go to dinner. If the robbery had taken place and anyone had died, I might be wearing orange prison garb. And a woman like you (though not you since you would not have been born) might have reported our captures on television, might have referred to your father and me as terrorists.

As relieved as I feel about not needing to play my part in the holdup, I always feel more emotion at your father thinking I had refused because I was incapable of an extraordinary act. Whenever they pop into my mind, his words *you won't* break me. But that isn't the point at this moment. What I'm wondering is how I can know you so well, you, the face on the television, the woman with the microphone and scarf, and you not know me at all?

Honey, our reservations are for seven.

I know. I'm just watching the end of the news.

Another bombing?

Yes. Lucy MacGiolla is reporting. Devon's daughter.

That quieted him. He walked up behind me, stood in reverence, and placed his hand on my shoulder. He knows the story—or thinks he knows the story. I told him all the relevant words before we married, but the story was from the country of my past, a place he never lived. A place that even I can't reenter, a place where you, the face on the television, are not just a former lover's child. You are the little girl I might have had, sitting side by side with my ghost daughter, on a branch in that vast forest of invisible family trees, the ones that no one ever talks about.

Maternal Instinct

Mostly I remember fragments. Flashes. The feel of my right shoe slipping, losing my foothold, my spine arching, then a rush of concrete and green. My elbow scraping a wall. Leaves and twigs scratching my cheek. Though I must have fallen twelve feet, I don't remember landing, making contact with the hard concrete bed beneath the artificial stream. I don't remember making a splash. My wrist stung above my left hand where I automatically tried to break the fall, but I didn't cry. I told myself, *Boys don't cry.*

I do remember squatting in the middle of the shallow stream, the dank feel of water, slimy water, not like the bath or the beach. A rustling sound. I remember looking around, knowing that I had landed in a different world.

~

I've had counselors over the years. Some said the trauma affected my memory, others said few people remember whole scenarios from when they were five, yet even as they dismissed my partial amnesia as natural, they all, at some point, pressed me to remember. I didn't like the way they asked, as if they were curious in a salacious way; they didn't want to help me, they wanted the story. A linear narrative. I refused to see any more therapists after my last counselor, the one I had when I was fifteen, the one who wanted to try hypnosis. My parents argued about it. My father wanted me to continue; my mother felt it was up to me. *If he doesn't want to go, it won't do any good. Besides, hypnosis is hocus-pocus.* She had been opposed to therapy from the start; in fact she had argued vehemently against it, saying the fall was just an accident, there was nothing to glean from therapy. *Besides,* she said, *I was there; I can tell you what happened.*

My father felt guilty that he hadn't been with us that day at the zoo. My mother was left alone to handle the three of us while he was moving into his colleague's apartment (he called her *colleague*; my mother called her *mistress*, or once, when she was really on edge, *whore*). My older brother, Willy, at eight, was three years my senior, and Ana was under a year old. My mother took us to the zoo because she couldn't stand to watch Dad carry out his possessions. Uncle Ty and Grandpa had stayed at the house to make sure Dad only removed his personal belongings. When I learned this detail, I felt sorry for Dad, imagining him taking hangers with shirts dangling off the rack while Grandpa and Uncle Ty, glaring, stood behind him, their arms crossed like barroom bouncers.

I didn't know any of this at the time. I don't even remember being particularly aware that Dad wasn't at the zoo that day. My mom and dad told me the full story after a therapy session the year before I stopped going. Mom explained what happened. I presume the therapist told them to tell me. I sat in the wing chair by the fireplace; they sat together on the couch, the yellow-and-pink-and-green floral upholstered one we had back then. Chintz. The sofa we had moved with us from the Midwest to the Northwest coast.

"Ana was fussing. Willy had run off to get a snow cone—it was so hot that day. The concrete wall surrounding the pit was about five feet high. I had had to lift you up onto the wall for you to see inside the pit. I knew it was a deep drop, but there was a railing on top of the wall. I had just set you down when Ana started screeching and I leaned down to her in the stroller. It was less than a minute. I was still vaguely aware of you out of the corner of my eye—and, of course, I knew about the railing. You must have leaned too far or stepped over it. I guess your sneaker slipped. I didn't see the second you went over. I was watching Ana. I heard a woman scream . . ." and then Mom burst into tears. "I shouldn't have looked away. I shouldn't have . . ."

Dad cupped his hand over hers.

"It's not your fault, Natalie. I should have been there." With his hand still over Mom's, he told me that they had been having problems, that he had foolishly thought he was in love with a colleague. He said he and Mom had gotten married young. He had been selfish. But he assured me that the moment he heard what happened, he had rushed to the hospital. He didn't tell me I was his favorite, but we all knew. I'm the one who looks like him. I have Dad's middle name. I'm the athletic, bookish boy. I have dark, thick hair, a furrow in my brow. Ana and Willy both look like Mom, fair and freckled. They are both more musical and liked math better than reading. They both needed braces. My mother never had her teeth fixed; they still protrude. Mine are perfect and straight, like Dad's. Dad's an attorney, and I'm in my first year of law school.

They told me he didn't return to his colleague's apartment for almost a week, and then he went only to reclaim his belongings.

I nodded and said, *That's okay. I wasn't really hurt. Just a broken wrist and a few scratches.*

It's not okay, said Dad.

I didn't tell them what I remembered after landing in the stream.

~

One second, I had been with my family, among crowds of pressing sweaty people, and the next second I was squatting in the stream, my shoes and socks saturated, my bottom wet. People shouting. I looked up and saw the mother gorilla slumping toward me, her long arms swinging, her curled knuckles sweeping the ground. I was not scared. I did not sense danger. I had seen gorillas in movies, cartoons and books. I loved *Curious George* and *Good Night, Gorilla*.

I remembered she moved toward me like a huge stuffed animal. A baby gorilla was riding on her back, its head looking over the mother's shoulder. I was happy. I had fallen inside a magical world, away from the oppressive heat and crowds. I later learned that the mother gorilla's name was Pebbles. The baby's name was Bamm-Bamm. They were one of the main zoo attractions because Bamm-Bamm had been born in captivity six months earlier. Pebbles arrived beside me quickly. Bamm-Bamm climbed down from her back and stood beside her mother. I know the crowd above the pit roared and screamed (I have seen video footage) but at that moment the noise of the crowd was a distant din. What I heard more clearly was a *who who who* sound from Bamm-Bamm and a cross between a growl and a meow from Pebbles. Neither sounded unfriendly. Pebbles took another step toward me. The three of us formed a tight circle. I looked up into Pebbles's golden eyes and she looked down into mine. We connected. Staring out from under deep brows, her glare was intense, yet kind, and concerned. In a flash, I was in her head and she in mine. At the time, I could only feel her thoughts. Now I can piece them together, put them into words.

Another baby, another one to care for, to cuddle, another one to protect. Where is its fur? Where did it come from, not from inside of me, no pain, no breaking apart down there like last time, but it is mine. Two babies to ride my back, to nurse, two babies to love, two babies to wrestle with each other. Warm, sweet, soft. This feels familiar, long ago, another place, another time, a deeper stream, I have seen this before—where? —another baby, my sister, my brother, a family again, another baby. Only hairy like us. Running in tall savannah grasses. Birds calling.

I shivered and tried to stand. The slimy water coated my hands and shorts. I wore my favorite Star Wars T-shirt, a hand-me-down from Will. The faces above us roared. The gorilla lifted her massive arm as if to pet me and I heard a loud explosion. In a flash, Pebbles became a mound of fur, her eyes no longer visible.

I don't remember how they removed me from the pit or the ambulance ride to the hospital, though I do remember the hospital bed with the silver arms that moved up and down. I remember the deep-red Jell-O they served, and I remember both my parents by my bedside. In the beginning I didn't tell them about my connection with Pebbles because no one asked and even if they had, I did not know how to explain how I traveled into her head, how I knew the gorilla's thoughts in her final moment, how I knew things about her life and her world that no five-year-old could. Later I didn't think people would believe me, and even if they did, to give away Pebbles's final thoughts felt like a betrayal of her last, most vulnerable moment in captivity, even worse than being christened a cartoon character's name.

My family suffered the year following the incident. Animal rights activists blamed my mother for not keeping better track of her children. My father was criticized for deserting a family with three small children. They received death threats. Editorials were written. Psychiatrists on talk shows said that both observers of the event and those who read about it on talk shows needed to compose narratives, construct explanations that helped them make sense of the event—to do so was a natural human urge. Kids at school called my brother Monkey Boy Bro and Gorilla Killa Kin. Only being in kindergarten, I was somewhat sheltered from these taunts, but was aware that our family had been greatly shamed because of me. After gentle persuasion, my father left his firm, and we moved where he got a position with a smaller, less lucrative practice.

After that, I would have to say that I had a pretty normal childhood. I didn't tell my new friends in Seattle about the incident. No one told me I couldn't, but it seemed a tacit agreement that we should not talk about the incident outside the family. Even in the family, the subject was more or less taboo. In high school, I was the captain of my school's soccer team. I was a member of the rock-climbing club. I had lots of friends but felt too ashamed to tell any of them about the defining moment of my childhood. In college whenever a new girlfriend and I shared our pasts I considered myself a fraud for failing to reveal the biggest event of mine: *Oh, yeah, and there's that time I fell into the gorilla pit at the zoo and survived, and made headlines all over the country. Maybe you heard about it?* In my last year of college, I told my first serious girlfriend, thinking that I needed to share my worst moment in order to be intimate, and she laughed; she thought I was joking. I wanted to break up with her but didn't think I could—once I convinced her of the veracity of my tale, she promised not to tell anyone, but I think she would have found our pact invalid if we were no longer a couple. So I stayed with her longer than I wanted. I ended it with her right after graduation and vowed to myself not to tell another woman unless we planned to wed. And I doubted I would marry, given I never wanted to have children. I was like the guys who didn't want to tell their partners that they had been arrested for drugs or joyriding or had a bipolar parent or been a total nerd in high school. Yet my secret was bigger, bigger even than what I have told you so far.

In most ways, we are a happy family. As far as I know, my father never cheated again. He became a devoted family man who spent all his free time with his wife or his children. My father and I still go rock-climbing together. Willy, Ana, and I are all good kids, unusually close siblings, even now that Willy is married. None of us ever got in trouble any more serious than talking back or being issued a parking ticket. My mother is less involved, more distant, than my father, particularly now that we are grown. But she usually takes our side in minor controversies and then Dad generally caves. Guilt, I suppose.

I didn't realize until recently how much more attractive my father is than my mother, but it is the kind of thing others—people outside the family—might have noticed. The sort of difference my father himself might have recognized when he found himself thirty-four years old and saddled with three small children, which was his age and situation when he tried to run off with his colleague. My father is a good man and cares greatly for my mother. I know everyone says looks shouldn't make a difference, but if you think about it, most people in a couple are pretty much equal on the attractiveness scale. It took Willy to do the math and point out my mother must have been four months pregnant when my parents married. None of these things are serious issues. Except for my brief encounter with the gorillas, our family problems appear typical of any loving family.

~

I went back to the scene of the crime by myself last year, between college and law school. I had been back to the Midwest before of course, to visit my grandparents, but no one ever suggested the zoo and I really had no way to get there on my own or explain my absence (as you might imagine, we are no longer a zoo-going family). The old outdoor gorilla pit had been replaced by a huge enclosure: twenty-foot glass walls on three sides, concrete on the fourth, and open on the top. A faux-rock tunnel led through the concrete wall to the gorillas' indoor quarters. I noted that most of the new jungle verisimilitude was for appearance, for the audience, not authentic enough for the gorillas. Painted jungle scenes sprawled the concrete wall. Brilliant yellow bananas. Nothing the gorillas could smell or taste. I imagined a fat tongue pressed against the dust-layered paint.

I watched the gorillas for a very long time. It was a cool day, so the gorillas were active, climbing and swinging on the two tires hung from poles. Despite the pleasant weather, the place smelled of shit; I don't recall that smell from when I was five even though it had been hot that day. I imagine in the real jungle, the stench is absorbed by the earth and plants and vastness.

I have to admit, I didn't recognize you, Bamm-Bamm. I thought I would, but I didn't, so I waited until a zookeeper happened along and I asked him if he knew which gorilla was which. The man wore faded-gray trousers and a matching shirt with the name *Tony* stitched above the pocket in red. He pointed you out and told me the story of your mother's death. I gasped and acted surprised. I asked for more details. He said I could still see the footage on YouTube. He told me the mother of the child had been investigated and cleared of negligence, a fact I had not heard previously but one that gave me a small sense of satisfaction.

"Everyone's cameras had been pointed at the pit," said Tony. "Not the boy's family. It was before everyone had cell phones. Only one guy had a videocam."

Tony said that Bamm-Bamm had never been able to mate in captivity. I have read a lot about gorillas and knew that male silverbacks were usually bred at fifteen. Since the incident had occurred about seventeen years earlier, I had a pretty good idea of Bamm-Bamm's age.

"I don't think the zoologists or the scientists would agree with me, but I think he didn't want a family of his own after he witnessed what happened to his mother." The man had thick, hairy eyebrows, like tarantulas clinging above his lids.

"Makes sense to me," I said. At that moment, I wanted to tell him who I was and ask his forgiveness, explain. I wanted to tell him that I was studying law to work on animal rights and defend activists. He seemed like a kindred spirit. I wanted to tell him about the connection I had with your mother, Bamm-Bamm. I wanted to tell him the secrets I had not told anyone up until now. But I felt I owed my confession to you—and you alone—even if it only meant writing it all out on this piece of paper, reading it aloud, and then burning the paper. I had hoped to drop it in the stream, but there was no access to it with those glass walls.

My mother need not have worried about what I would have told therapists, because I would never tell a single human about what happened right before my shoe slipped. I would never tell how I remembered the pressure of the heel of my mother's hand in the small of my back, the way the palm rolled to the fingertips, the gentle but definitive shove. I never will tell anyone besides you. I can't claim to know why she did it. Because I looked so much like my father? Because she thought the tragedy would bring him back? Was she so crazed at being abandoned with three small children that she didn't know what she was doing? An unchecked impulse. Or is it possible that—like the shrinks say—I created a narrative to make sense of the event, to make myself a victim who could forgive and protect his mother? I can't say with absolute certainty because of all the flashes recalled from that day, my mother's hand on my back is not the most distinct. What remains strongest is my exchange with your mother, the love and concern she exhibited in her last moments. I can honestly say I have never felt such an immediate and powerful connection. As for my mother, if she did what I think, I need to convey to you—as well as man can to ape—that as tragic as you mother's death was, the sacrifice was not all in vain. Your family was lost so mine could be saved.

JUMP

Even though we weren't supposed to cut through the industrial corridor on our way home from church, we did. It was quicker, and there was a big space between the foundry and the chicken-boxing factory to practice. No one was there on a Sunday. We had the vast space to ourselves. Janelle and I were the second- and third-best jump-ropers in the fifth grade, right after Marcia Mims. We knew all the rhymes and most of the tricks.

It's not easy for two girls to practice with one rope, but I wasn't allowed to take mine to church. Janelle took hers everywhere, like a sharpshooter who couldn't be without her gun, the handle sticking out of her pocket, a pistol in its holster. With seven kids, her mother couldn't keep track of what they all did. I envied her rope, twisted yellow-and-red twine with thin, red handles. Mine was just the regular color of rope with varnished, brown-wood handles.

My mother didn't care for Janelle, but what could she do? We were best friends, went to the same school and church, and only lived four houses away. I don't think my mother would disapprove of her for being poorer—nine of them stuffed into the same-style small house as ours, which often felt too crowed for us five. She wasn't a money snob. It's not like we were rich. Maybe it was because their yard was a mess—old, rusting junk and broken plastic toys, soaked fliers never collected and thrown away. And Janelle usually did seem grimy. She was only allowed a bath every other night unless she and her oldest sister shared the tub, which her sister usually refused. We were both skinny with short hair but mine was neater. My mother used Scotch tape to keep my bangs even when she trimmed. Janelle's older sister cut hers with *what looked like hedge clippers*, my mother said. And poor Janelle had to wear her sister's wool tights, so large they draped on her legs like elephant skin.

That day, folding her long rope once over to shorten it, we took turns—closer to the foundry because the asphalt outside the chicken factory was slick with grease, unusual for a Sunday—doing solitary jumps. They must have been working overtime. Then we each took an end and practiced twirling the rope as fast as we could, preparing for Marcia at school. *I am a pretty little Dutch Girl!* I was so focused on the swish and slap—over and over—that the man with the camera was almost upon us before I turned and spotted him, snapping photos. He startled me into a smile. He was younger than our parents but older than the high school boys. He kept circling us, clicking his black camera. I said *No, stop,* but he kept going. I dropped my end of the rope. The man paused and—offering up his fancy camera—said, *Let me show you this contraption.*

His black hair was combed to the far-right side, plastered down, and his eyes were trimmed in such broad lashes that they reminded me of sunflowers.

We're not allowed to talk to strangers, I said. *Com'on, Janelle, let's go.*

Janelle brushed me away and stepped closer to him. Without forethought, I took off in the opposite direction in a gallop, looking back only once to see Janelle's thin, white neck bent over the camera as he pointed to different gears and gadgets.

She didn't come to school for days, and when she did, she stayed inside during recess to help Mrs. Cornell clean the boards. It must have been a month—but who knew time in those days? —before she sought me out. She carried an old and peeling patent leather purse.

Look what I got, she said and pulled out a five-by-five black and white of us twirling the rope. It looked crisper and more professional than any photo I had ever seen. In it, Janelle and I were separated by the spinning rope, going so fast that it was barely a visible blur, as if the two of us would never be fully connected again.

My Practice Life

The summer my niece, Heidi, turned six years old, I developed a daily true-false observation quiz for her.

We saw four dogs on leashes at the park	T	F
My aunt's ice cream cone was chocolate	T	F
I never feel sad	T	F

She loved the game and always got one hundred percent, never noticing that some questions (Birds sing when they are happy) had no one correct answer. For me, the game provided a means of entrée into her mood, a way to ask questions about topics and emotions she avoided. Heidi's mother had died of an aggressive form of breast cancer when Heidi was only three. When Heidi was out of school for the summer and I was off as well (I was a teacher), she lived with me while my younger brother (her father) worked. My own husband, Ron, died in a car accident just a few years after we wed, so I knew about hiding emotions.

As Heidi got older, we continued with the quiz, though I had to be more cunning with the trick questions—and more original with observational ones: "We saw three women with alien-like face-lifts today T F."

We shared a common view of the world. Irreverent. Cynical. Or what Heidi's psychiatrist called—in her case, not mine—highly defended. I thought the quiz kept her in the moment. Studious, a reader, she liked tests, particularly since I told her they were only practice, not for credit. When she asked to take the real test, I would make up a new one and type it out (the practice tests were verbal) or tell her that she had done so well on the practice test that she had been excused. I always believed we were getting over our traumas together and once she grew up, we would emerge changed, on the other side of sorrow, together.

We spent every holiday break together and half of each summer, usually at my house in Chicago. Her father joined us for most of the time in the early years. Certainly for Christmas. That stopped when Heidi was in high school and he remarried. His new life didn't have much room for

Heidi. I was sorry for her, to lose another parent. But in some ways we were more comfortable, just us females. We enjoyed decorating the tree and sunning on the Oak Street Beach in the summer. Her father had no patience for that.

I was delighted when following college, Heidi moved to Chicago for graduate school. We spent at least one night a week together. We called the nights our "bonding sessions." Not that we needed artificial bonding, given we had been irrevocably bonded by circumstance so early in her life. Often we went out to dinner or a movie, but we loved events that seemed less ordinary. We were always scouring the newspapers and posters at the El stations.

Heidi had just started work on her dissertation when we attended the Past Life Regression Workshop. Oh, I know, that sounds a bit nutty or new age, whereas my niece and I are anything but. Most likely we would be categorized as staunch realists who wished the world had not forced us into such roles. We expected nothing from the workshop except a few laughs, perhaps some material (from the leader, the other participants) to poke fun at afterward. But secretly we thought it would be nice if the workshop was able to reveal that we had been Joan of Arc or Lady Godiva in our previous lives. We joked about it. Heidi said that she could see me as Joan of Arc. I had been the most active in defending our school principal when I thought she was being unfairly dismissed, and I fought long and hard against the increase in standardized testing at the middle school where I taught. Though my remarks about sexism in the firing of the principal had been quoted in the *Sun Times*, my intervention had no impact and was certainly not the result of divine guidance. I told Heidi that if she grew out her wavy, shoulder-length hair, she would look lovely on a white horse. She threw her head back to laugh. I loved that mannerism of hers. Though I didn't share it with Heidi, I secretly thought it would be even nicer if instead of going back to former lives, we could do go back earlier in our current lives for a do-over. Wouldn't it have been nice if I had told my husband, Ron, not to go into work that day or to watch out for red trucks on his way home? (I'm not sure what Heidi could have done differently except find out that her mother had been misdiagnosed.) Even nicer to go back and find out all the horrendous things that had happened to us were just practice lives, like practice tests, that could be wiped out entirely to make way for more opportunities when we entered our *real* lives. We were too cynical (or, maybe, it made us too sad) to discuss any of that much.

The workshop cost a mere twenty dollars and took place at a recreation center housed about two blocks from where I live in Lincoln Park. The center usually offered crafts classes or flamenco dancing, that sort of thing. I had never been before and usually threw out the newsprint fliers the place stuffed under my door. My niece saw the workshop advertised online.

"The instructor is certified," she said when she called me to tell me about it. She couldn't hide the smile in her tone.

"You sure it didn't say *certifiable?*"

"It's BYOC."

"Huh?"

"Bring your own candle."

The class description actually included the candle—not the acronym, my niece invented that, but the candle part was real. Did the flickering candles help one enter the distant past or just make the whole experience feel more transcendental?

The temperature hovered slightly above zero the evening of the workshop. We walked the two icy blocks taking pigeon steps, our arms linked, trying not to slip. Heidi clutched a heavy brown paper lunch bag that held her broad candle. I carried my slightly used tapered dinner candle in my purse. In comparison to her fat candle, mine seemed ridiculously delicate. How would it even stand on its own with no holder? I felt I had already failed the workshop. As a former science teacher before retiring, there was little I disliked more than an unprepared student. I could sympathize with students who had difficulty understanding the concepts, but not with the ones who had not even tried to complete the homework. I had to remind myself that the past life regression workshop was no-credit.

Heidi lived in a less expensive part of the city than I, so she took the bus over to walk with me. I lived in what some would deem a ritzy part of the city. Upon my husband's death, I received significant proceeds from his life insurance that I invested wisely and didn't touch until my retirement. Public school teachers in Chicago are allowed to retire after twenty years. I waited an extra five years. I rewarded myself by moving and paying cash for the fancy graystone.

The lobby of the recreation center was not impressive. Cracking plaster walls. Peeling linoleum. Water spots spreading like continents on the ceiling. A group of giggling ten-year-olds in leotards blocked our way to a long folding table with a woman seated in a chair behind it.

"Girls, girls, make way," said the woman. She had bottle-brown hair hanging from an inch of white along the part line. It reminded me that I was past due at the hair salon. I also thought of it as a possible test question for Heidi. I still gave her the true-false tests, though not as frequently. Rather than a means of testing her mood, I hoped for her to throw her head back in a laugh. The woman took our registration slips and told us our class was on the second floor.

"The elevator is broken," she said, tilting her head in the direction of a long and steep stairway to the left. Ever since we had started navigating the slippery sidewalks, my mood had been shifting between irritated and hopeful. Her words weighted it more in the direction of irritation. I took a deep breath and clung to the railing as we climbed.

Six other participants already sat in folding chairs arranged in a semicircle in the large rectangular fluorescent-lit room where the workshop was to take place. One entire long wall was mirrored and outfitted with a dance bar. Since I felt slightly out of breath from the stairs, I briefly hoped that I might have been a dancer in a former life and would spring into movement. A slight distance from the semicircle, in the widest opening, sat the man whom I assumed was the instructor. He was bone-thin and sat cross-legged on the seat of his chair. Piled beside him on a slightly wobbly table (I assume it traveled with him from workshop to workshop) were books, papers, and several objects I couldn't discern. On the floor in front of his chair sat a hydrant-sized candle. From the look of most of our classmates—most in their late twenties or early thirties, well-dressed, good haircuts—I assumed that they, like us, were cynics, here for a laugh. At this realization, I felt sympathy for the instructor who appeared—with his table of class supplies and the gigantic, already-lit candle—to be serious.

He instructed Heidi and me to get chairs from the stacks at the far end of the room.

As I set up my chair, I surreptitiously studied the instructor's face. Who taught past-life regression courses at a disintegrating community center? He was about my age, perhaps a few years younger. I could tell from his crystal-blue eyes and aquiline nose that he must have been strikingly handsome before he lost his hair. Not that I find balding men unattractive. It was his particular form of baldness: totally shiny skull—gleaming under the fluorescent lights—except for a dark, round peninsula of hair that jutted out over his frontal lobe and a thin ring wrapped around the back of his head from ear to ear. Just a little hair would have drastically changed his appearance.

"Take out your candles please." He frowned and sighed. "The center was supposed to supply a seminar table for us to put them on but someone forgot and the supply room locks at five, so you will need to put them on the floor in front of you, maybe a foot away."

I wedged my candle between my purse and my date book. I hoped it wouldn't topple.

"Does anyone have an extra candle?" asked a woman with a carefully tussled haircut and a series of tiny hoop earrings lining the rim of her right ear like the spine of a spiral notepad.

"I do," said Heidi, pulling two fat candles from her bag and passing one to the woman. I gave Heidi a look and she twisted her mouth in an impish smile. I realized that—joke or not—she was aiming to be class pet. In a corner of my brain, I began to construct the quiz:

The woman who needed a candle had eight rings on one ear	T	F
The woman collecting registration slips dyed her hair	T	F
We took the class more seriously than we planned	T	F

As I draped my coat on the back of my chair, I noticed the room was quite chilly. I assumed they were saving on their gas bill, not actually trying to create an atmosphere more conducive to ghosts and time travel.

"Two more people are enrolled," said the instructor. "We'll just wait a few minutes for them to arrive. In the meantime, let's go around the room and introduce ourselves. I'll go first. Please call me Alfonso. I have been conducting past life regression excursions for almost ten years and also work in hypnosis, meditations and teach yoga."

I was stuck on his hair. I could see how before he lost it he must have been the type of guru who attracted young women and older widows, which would qualify both Heidi and me. His areas of work were perfect for meeting women. Had his hair loss slowed him down? As I wondered about the instructor's motives and prospects, my husband Ron's face floated into view. I could no longer remember what he looked like when I tried to conjure his features, and then, when least expecting it, his face would appear full force, every detail: his scruffy auburn hair, the left eye slightly larger than the right, the fullness of his lower lip, the crescent-shaped scar on his chin. The image never remained for more than a few seconds.

"Please give your name and tell why you're taking the class."

Most of the other women said they thought the class would be interesting or fun. The only true kook in the group, Gwyneth, said she had traveled back to many of her past lives on her own but decided that to go even further she needed a class. Her head was shaved except for a Tintin-like tuft in the front that was dyed magenta. She wore a long, black dress, a magenta shawl that matched her hair, and clunky hiking boots. I imagined her to be about my age. We were the oldest two in the room. No men besides the instructor. Gwyneth told us about some of her other lives, Alfonso nodding along. I noted they were all famous people—queens and kings, Christopher Columbus, and Mary Todd Lincoln. Weren't people ever day laborers or homeless in their former lives?

"Oh my God, that night at the theater, when Abe's head slumped to my shoulder. That was the worst night of that life." She put her head in her hands; the magenta tuft quivered as she shook her head back and forth. When she looked back up, her eyes were moist. The two women sitting next to her nudged each other.

Heidi's turn was next.

"My name is Heidi, and I have always felt that I've lived previously and thought the best way to access a former life would be to seek the guidance of a professional in the field."

I think I audibly groaned before I followed with the completely uninspired response of, "My name is Julia and my niece, Heidi, suggested I take the class with her."

"Maybe the two people not here have decided it was too cold to go outside," said the woman with the earrings. "I say we get started. I don't know how long I'm going to last in this room. It's fucking freezing."

My sympathy for Alfonso increased; I felt sure that there had been a time in his life when his sessions were filled to standing room only and no one spoke disrespectfully. The seventies or eighties when people were into such things. Still, he complied with the request, telling us to light our candles. He rose and walked to the back of the room to shut off the lights. When he returned to his seat, his face was underlit, the shadow of his nose dancing as he told of his own past lives. His voice sank deeper, became echoic, as if drifting up from a well. He said he had been shot and killed in the Civil War. After the battle, during the body count, just as his soul was departing, he heard them say his name. Ambrose Johnson. More recently (meaning over a hundred years later), he had researched Ambrose Johnson and found out he had been killed at Gettysburg.

"I wonder if Abe ever met you," said Gwyneth. I didn't look at Heidi for fear of laughing.

"I was just a foot soldier," said Alfonso. He smiled and continued talking. A handsome man's smile, one that could be taken as reaffirming or condescending, depending on the viewer's inclination. The story of Ambrose Johnson's life was not particularly interesting, but I discerned it was building to some grand conclusion, which turned out to be the remarkable coincidence that both men had the same initials. Also, both of their mothers were named Amelia.

And—the coup de grâce—Alfonso had managed to find a daguerreotype of Ambrose standing with a group of fellow soldiers in front of a tent.

"I've had it blown up," he said. He gently pulled a sheet of stiff paper about sixteen inches by sixteen from a folder and passed it around. "It's a little blurry, but I'm sure you can see the resemblance."

The edges of the sheet felt soft as flannel from years of handling.

Ambrose's face was circled with a red grease pencil. I have to admit it *did* resemble the person named Alfonso who sat in front of us, though younger and more handsome given his thick head of hair. That said, the image was blurry enough that it probably looked like thousands of men. What is a face except two eyes, a nose, and a mouth?

After all of us had sufficiently oohed and ahhed over the similarity between the two men (Heidi more than most), Alfonso told us several stories of people he had helped to regress and the coincidences among their current lives and their past lives. A man whose hobby it was to build ships in bottles had been a sea captain. A dog trainer who had died from the bite of a rabid dog in a former life. That sort of thing. Many had ethnic similarities to the people they were in their former lives. Many looked like their former personhood. He had a few other examples to show us. Photocopied photos of people from the past alongside photos of more recent clients. There were vague familiarities between the people. He explained that he did not have more because not every former life could be recorded and researched. And, he warned us, past names were not always available in regressions.

I had to conclude that he was not a charlatan or he would have had more dramatic stories, more famous people. He believed what he said. I suspected that—given the sense of trust he conveyed—at one time in his life, others had believed him as well. I wondered how much longer his career could last as he continued to age and give classes to fewer and fewer reverent students. That was one reason I retired. I didn't want to become the old woman pulling a crinkled tissue out of my dress sleeve while students snickered. I felt sad thinking how a once charismatic man was so likely to end up alone.

Would Ron have lost his hair? The thought had never occurred to me before, though I had often wondered if he would have received tenure. We moved to Chicago for a position at the University of Chicago. There was no dual appointment for me, so I took the job as the middle school teacher. I didn't mind. Our plan was to have children as soon as he acquired tenure. We even had imaginary names for them. At the time, women with children were much less likely to acquire tenure. Besides, I knew I wasn't as good a scientist as Ron. He was obsessed. The week he died he had barely ate or slept. I am certain he was thinking of a grant application deadline the night he turned left into the red truck. The accident was probably his fault, though his culpability was blurred by the fact that the other driver had been drinking.

Heidi elbowed me, and when I glanced over, she shot out a breath that actually created a little cloud in the air. The room was that cold.

We were instructed to close our eyes, to keep them closed, to let our minds drift. Alfonso said nothing for what must have been a full five minutes. I shivered and pulled my coat around my shoulders and peeked. Everyone else had their eyes closed. Heidi even had her head thrown back. Her bottom lip hung open. Heidi had been a pretty child, oddly like the Little Golden Book version of the character for whom she was named, with apple cheeks, wide eyes and wavy, blond hair. Her hair had darkened with age and her eyes had become more focused, intense.

I reclosed my eyes.

"Go back, back, tumble back in time, to when you were in school, grade school, remember your desk, look at your hands holding crayons, the playground, go back, back, back in time." His voice deepened and droned, different from the voice he had used when his eyes were open. The echo quality had turned into a humming vibration, the words blurring together. *"Back, back, back to when you first learned to walk, pulling yourself up."*

The cold was making the effort difficult but I actually tried. I recalled my teaching days—making paper-mache and baking soda volcanoes for the children—my graduate school days, the scratched wooden desks of my own elementary school. I cannot describe how long Alfonso went on in this droning manner without making my own story impossibly boring. Just take my word that each stage of our lives received detailed attention.

"*Before you could walk, drift, drift, keep going. You are crawling.*"

I imagined little hands on a floor, wooden boards, looking up to see the corner of a table.

"*Further, back, back, in your crib, see the bars. You want to get out but you are going back, farther, you are no longer drifting, you are being pulled back, you are curled in a ball, tumbling through a dark tunnel, you are crying, screaming, you have just come into the light, and now you are back in darkness.*"

At some point his voice turned into a steady buzz, an inhuman sound, neither high nor low, though not uncomforting.

Hmmmmmmmm.

I recalled the fiancé I had had briefly the year Heidi turned fifteen, the summer her father remarried and she had been so much trouble. She gave herself a choppy haircut, dyed it tar-black, and ran away. It was the only time I recall her being difficult. Still, her behavior certainly scared off my fiancé. Or at least that's what I thought frightened him. After Heidi returned, while he and I waited in the police station for her to be processed, he said he didn't think he wanted children. I wasn't quite forty yet but my clock was ticking. In retrospect, I think if I had put forth some effort, I could have made him stay, talked him into a family. Yet it somehow seemed disloyal to Ron to fight to keep this fiancé who said he didn't want children. More important, it seemed almost as if my life with Ron had been a different life than the one that I was leading at that moment, which suggested there were more lives to come in my future. And finally, I believed I would always have my students and Heidi. How strange that at that time, in my late thirties, it had never really occurred to me that I could end up alone.

My thoughts about Ron, the fiancé began to drift.

Hmmmmmmmm.

I continued to sit in Alfonso's presence, in the large room in the city, dark except for the glow of candles, but I found myself in another room as well. I reclined in an antique sleigh bed under a window with fluttering white eyelet curtains. Outside the countryside sprawled, ripples of verdant hills. My head sunk in the pillow. I could not lift it to see the hills, but my spirit floated above my body and I could remember the hills, running on them when I was a girl. The body in the bed was old, frail, with bluish-white translucent skin. I knew she (I) was dying. Where was everyone? I was by myself, a blanket pulled up over my cold breasts, my arms resting on top of the blanket. Had I not had children in my previous life either?

Someone coughed.

"Wow. That was something."

I opened my eyes to see the speaker was the woman with the ear lined in little rings speaking.

"I was a flapper at a party. I had on the coolest sequined dress."

"I was a man," said another woman. "Driving some kind of carriage or taxi, I think. It was horse-drawn."

"I was the leader of a group of cave people," said Gwyneth. "I invented fire."

Was this for real? I wondered. Could any—Gwyneth aside—of these people believe what they were saying? Didn't they understand the power of suggestion? I thought my vision of the woman in her bed must have just been imagined, a place my mind drifted. How could it not be, as I had never lost awareness of the community center room or Alfonso as I floated above my bedridden body?

I turned to Heidi.

"What about you?" I asked, still remembering when her tar-colored hair was almost grown out, the tips like the paint-saturated ends of a paint brush.

"I was a pioneer woman in a snowstorm."

I twisted my lips in skepticism.

"No, really," she said. "I knew I wasn't going to make it in the blizzard."

Everyone excitedly exchanged stories. I did not tell of the woman in the bed by the window.

Instead, I said, "It was too cold for me to regress."

Afterward, as we gathered our belongings and prepared to reenter the truly freezing outdoor temperatures, Alfonso came over to Heidi and told her that he sometimes offered private excursions.

"Thank you," she said. "But I just got engaged. I'll be moving to the West Coast soon."

Alfonso gave Heidi his card anyway, which we later laughed about, as the printed phone number was crossed out, replaced by a second number also crossed out, then a third number. But that night as we walked back to my place for a glass of wine, she spoke energetically of the experience. I knew of the engagement, of course, but not of the move. I wondered if she had made up the move to get rid of Alfonso. I was more troubled by the fact that she seemed to have accessed a past life while I had failed.

~

That session happened a few years ago. Heidi is expecting her first child now. She followed in my footsteps in science. She has a university job on the West Coast, but things are different these days. When she became pregnant, they gave her extra time to complete her bid for tenure. Departments need women now.

Though we talk every week or two, I am a part of Heidi's past life now. Her former life. She has to regress to find me.

Given the evening was not recent, took up no more than two hours, and was intended as a lark, I think of it more frequently than I should. I wonder if the other women in the room, Heidi included, told the truth that night. And I wonder about the woman in the bed. Was she my imagination? If not, had I simply not gone back far enough to see the essence of her life, or did the lonely moment of her death define her? Most of all, I worry that the vibes in the room became confused, the mystical wires crossed, which resulted in time collapsing and me somehow—instead of traveling back— going forward to see my future, the only one I'll ever have. Could someone please compose a quiz for me, maybe a short answer instead of true-false, any type of quiz as long as it will help me finally get beyond this practice life?

The Goodbye Party

There were just the three of us bellied up to the bar that night: Holster. Blue Dog. And me. Not surprising since the town had just been dumped with a fresh twelve inches on top of the six we already had. The few cars out on Main Street were buried, just rounded lumps that looked like little igloos.

Given the inclement conditions, Raven served every other drink on the house. Not that she needed an excuse, since it was neither her bar nor her dough. She liked to drink with the patrons, and it seemed impolite to charge them for what she got for free. On the nights she worked, a lot of people waited until after eleven to arrive, since by that time she had passed the legal limit and her generosity really began to flow. That night, I suspected we would be the only customers, hence her early generosity. During the winter, without the tourists on their way to Yellowstone and with no need to staff the restaurants or the attractions, the town totaled only about eighty-five residents, and who but the regulars—the professionals, as we like to call ourselves—would venture out in such a blizzard?

The bar had a cozy feeling. With all the blown snow outside and the frost on the inside, the transparent section of the two front windows had shrunk to the size of portholes. The colored Christmas lights still strung behind the bar sparkled hopefully. In the back, the fridge with the glass door—which opened to milk and eggs and whatnot for the folks who had not had the forethought to drive from Doe Ridge into Warren and stock up—glowed and hummed comfortably. No matter how bad it got, we weren't going to starve.

The thing about Holster and Blue Dog was that they could talk about nothing for hours. Sometimes, in the summer when I had odd jobs to do, I would slap a five on the bar and leave when I got too tired of nebulous arguing about whether Blue Dog had bought his pickup in '97 or '98, or how long so-and-so had lived in his cabin. But that night the nothing-talk, like the glow and purr of the fridge, felt reassuring, as if the whole world could be smothered in white and we would continue existing in our own warm and iridescent cocoon.

I listened while Blue Dog debated the virtues of cutting his hair. It had hung past his shoulders for over two decades, since he was in his twenties, and was still reasonably thick. This debate had persisted for about five years, from the time Holster had cut off his. Holster had tried to donate it to a place that makes wigs for cancer victims but they rejected it.

"They'd probably take yours," said Holster. "I should'a washed mine before I cut it." I didn't volunteer that his hair had gotten so wispy that they would have needed fifty ponytails of the same heft to make a wig for a five-year-old. I don't know how he even managed to get such a pathetic little tail into a rubber band without ripping it out.

"It just seems like I'd be kowtowing to the times if I got it cut now. Lose a part of my individuality," said Blue Dog. Blue Dog raised dogs and horses and had an animal training business. He was smart, though I don't think he ever went to college. But he got stuck on little things, so it took people a while to recognize his intelligence. He had only two dogs when I first met him; now he bred them so fast I couldn't keep count, and he kept eight horses of his own for breeding and renting out to tourists in the summer. A real entrepreneur. He was the only one of us who had earned enough dough on his own to buy a place that was more than just a two- or three-room cabin with a postage-size patch of dirt. He must have had ten acres.

"You can't hang onto the past," said Holster. Holster lived in an old school bus that he had equipped (well, actually, Blue Dog had done it for him) with electricity by cutting into the power lines. We had all chipped in to dig a deep pit six feet behind the bus and build a wooden outhouse over it.

The barroom door swung inward, followed by a swirl of snow. I didn't need to glance up from my whiskey to know it was Sandy. But I did. He shoved the door shut and stomped his boots. Snow was encrusted on his stocking cap and in his bushy, red beard.

"Hell of a night," said Sandy, unzipping his coat and heading toward the bar.

"You check on Larkspur?" asked Holster.

Larkspur had been sick for a few weeks and we had been taking turns. His skin turned yellow a while back, and a few days ago his eyeballs had followed suit. The weather had been too bad to drive into the hospital in Bozeman. Besides, Larkspur had reasoned, he would either get better or worse, and if he got worse, he didn't want to die in a hospital. At forty-eight, Larkspur was a year younger than me, but like the rest of us, he had lived a life that tested the laws of longevity.

"He's gone," said Sandy. He reached the corner of the bar, hoisted a boot onto the brass footrail, and turned to Raven.

"The regular?" she asked, lifting a heavily penciled eyebrow.

"That'a do it," said Sandy. Unlike most of us, he had grown up in Montana, just three miles outside of town. He grew a beard every winter and shaved his face clean the first of every April. Sandy and his brother worked their father's ranch. Someday they would inherit it and be wealthy, but ranch-wealthy didn't buy a person any freedom from work.

"Where'd he go in this weather?" asked Blue Dog, spinning around on his stool to face Sandy.

"I mean *gone* gone, as in dead."

That shut down the banter.

My limbs froze, atrophied, and a charge shot through my brain, triggering a ripple that passed through my system, from my scalp to my toes. Even Raven paused midpour. If I could call any of them a best friend, it would have been Larkspur. We had both arrived in Doe Ridge the same year, had both dropped out of our respective colleges in our third year, and both came from middle-class families with mothers who stayed home and fathers who wore a suit and tie every day to nondescript middle-management jobs. I grew up playing board games with a brother in a faux-colonial house in Bethesda, and Larkspur and his two sisters did the same in a split-level in a suburb of Indianapolis.

"Dead?" I asked.

"Dead," said Sandy and forked his right hand up his neck, through his beard, fluffing it out from his chin. A few beads of icy water dripped onto the bar.

Raven poured us each a shot of Maker's Mark and hoisted hers.

"To Larkspur," we all said as we clicked our hard, little glasses.

No one spoke or asked any questions for quite a while.

"I just saw him this morning, and he seemed okay," said Blue Dog. "Were you there when he passed?"

What a peculiar term, I thought, *passed*. As if his ghost exited his body and sailed by Sandy on his way to where, I couldn't say.

Larkspur and I had both scoffed at the safe, predictable lives of our parents. We wanted adventures, but for a long time, we shared the tacit belief that we could—in fact, probably would—return to lives like those of our childhood at any time of our choosing.

"Nope. I just found him sitting there on his floor, all dressed, jeans and that green flannel shirt, propped against his armchair, his head up, legs spread, as natural as could be," said Sandy. "He's got stacks of old photos between his legs, like he knew what was going to happen, like he wanted one last look before he died."

Another reverent silence.

"Did you move him?" asked Blue Dog.

"He looked comfortable the way he was."

"Maybe we should call someone or something?" asked Raven.

"No one is coming to get him in weather like this. Let him be. His sisters live five hours away in good weather." It was the first time I had spoken.

We had another round. No one spoke for a long while. After all, it wasn't an emergency. We had all seen enough dead bodies not to question Sandy's diagnosis. What else was there to say? In comparison, Blue Dog's hair had been transformed into a frivolous subject.

I thought of the Sundays that Larkspur and I had sat on the porch of his cabin, doing the *New York Times* crossword. He was good with words, had been a classics major—to the same paternal disapproval that I had earned as a philosophy major, which gave us the vague notion that though we were a part of Doe Ridge, we were also separate from it, as if we had actually completed our degrees. No one else got the *Times*, let alone did crosswords.

Slapping his palms on the bar, Holster stood up.

"I'm going to pay my respects," said Holster. To me, it seemed more like he was simply going to view the body, in all its vulnerability. I didn't want to see it, to see the tableau in which Larkspur had ended his days.

Holster wrapped the thick, purple scarf that his last girlfriend had knitted for him (begun and completed the three weeks she lasted living in the school bus) around his neck. None of us were married, although everyone but me had been, at least once. I thought about how I would feel if I were sitting dead in my cabin and Holster—Blue Dog's sidekick, sometimes considered the town clown—came barging in, but it didn't seem my place to object. And though I would have liked to think otherwise, I suspected Larkspur hadn't passed to anywhere where he could feel anything now, one way or another. As Holster departed, the snow swirled in and the wind howled, then abruptly ceased when he slammed the door.

We were three again at the bar. But the feeling of comfort had vanished. I could sense Blue Dog being drawn toward the door. And sure enough, a shot and a beer later, he was off to pay his respects as well. Larkspur lived less than a half mile from the bar, on a road parallel to Main, though slightly up the ridge at the base of the mountains, so he could look down on the town. I lived at the opposite end of town, but also above it.

"I feel sort of responsible," said Sandy before Blue Dog had slipped on his gloves. Sandy threw back his shot, zipped up his jacket, and joined Blue Dog. "I mean, it's my shift—I should be there."

Many years ago, while "engaged" (whatever that means—it's not like we exchanged rings) to Raven's best friend, Carly, I spent thirty-seven hours in a hotel room with two college girls on their way to Yellowstone. While I was in the room, Raven and Carly slit all four tires on my truck. I could never prove they did it, but they knew and I knew. We had a cold war for a while, then Carly moved down to Jackson Hole, so holding spite against Raven seemed pointless. In a town this size, you need to be selective about how many grudges you want to carry and how many wars you're willing to wage. And I guess they did have provocation for slicing my tires. Now Raven and I were like siblings. In fact, most people in town of a certain age, particularly those of us who had moved out to Montana back then, the tail end of the so-called hippie era, seemed related.

"So, what ya thinking?" she asked. Except for the eyebrows, she didn't wear any makeup. Her face was just beginning to acquire that hard look that some mountain women got when they passed the age of forty-five: a firm jaw and a full facial map of little wrinkles, but only a few deep ones. As long as they didn't wear too much makeup and still wore their hair long, the look had a certain appeal, like the faces of wise little girls who had aged prematurely.

"You want to close up, don't you?" It wasn't quite midnight which meant, technically, she had over an hour to go. I didn't want to leave. It felt like if I sat there I would not have to face Larkspur, face the fact that we weren't all safe in our little cocoon. Besides, my limbs, especially my legs, felt paralyzed.

She leaned forward and peered up and down the bar, shading her eyes with her right hand like a sailor in a ship's crow's nest, in mock search of other customers.

"As much as I feel needed here and know that the tips will more than make up for the inconvenience of having to brush off the four more inches of snow that is bound to accumulate before closing, yes, I do want to close up early."

"What if someone needs milk?"

"I guess they should have fucking thought of that before now." I knew it was a losing battle, so I closed out my tab—which only showed two drinks of the five or six I had consumed—and told her I would wait while she finished up to help her scrape off her car. Anything to stall for time.

Raven got behind the wheel of her old green Honda to start the motor and let it heat up. When the light went on inside the car, the mound of snow took on the appearance of a candle in a frosted glass container, the light shimmering dully through the layers of snow. It was beautiful: a winter lantern. Once the car was running firmly, she stepped outside to join me, slamming the door so that the snow slid off the driver's window, ruining the effect of sheltered luminosity. We worked in silence for a few minutes. I liked sweeping the stratums into avalanches off the sides and backs of the car, and watching the white build on Raven's uncovered hair. I also liked the fact that our work helped me avoid the inevitable.

"Need a ride?" she asked when we were finished. "You can pick your truck up tomorrow."

"No, I think I'll stop by Larkspur's house first." I could no longer prevent time from moving forward. "You wanna come?"

She shook her head no, flinging snow from her hair. The light from the lamp behind her created the sense of a gauzy nimbus circling her head. I wanted her to beg me not to go, to come home with her to her tiny, yellow house, where she would hold me under heavy quilts, keeping us both anchored to the earth, until morning. After Carly had moved to Wyoming and Raven and I were trying to patch things up, I had slept there with her a few times. There was never the thought of us becoming a couple. It was more like an extended handshake to end the feud. I tried to remember if she and Larkspur had once been an item. He was—or at least had been— probably the best-looking man in town, tall with golden hair, broad shoulders, and a narrow waist. But about five years ago, he had lost a wing tooth beside his left front tooth that he didn't have the dough to cap, and, more recently, he had lost a little too much weight. The combination gave him a downtrodden look, robbing him of the appearance of his middle-class roots. I would be surprised if Raven hadn't been with him. He had lived in Doe Ridge since the day he had moved west from Indiana when he dropped out of college. With so few year-round residents, the idea of six degrees of separation suggested ridiculously distant connections. Most of us were separated by just a degree or two, sometimes a fraction of a degree, sometimes not at all. Not biologically, of course. But most of us had worked together at one time, lived next door, or been lovers or lovers of a lover.

There was a moment of eye contact before she slipped into her car. But she didn't beg; she didn't even ask.

Raven's Honda took off in a spray of pristine snow. Her car appeared to be nestled between the feathery white wings of a giant dove. I stared until she was consumed by the white shroud, and then started walking the opposite direction on Main Street. Sandy had plowed it, along with the path down the mountain from his dad's place. Nothing else was cleared, so I figured I would walk down Main until I was directly below Larkspur's, then cut up behind the backs of the shops. The snow on either side of the narrow rut rose so high that I felt like I was hiking a silt-filled river bed. Though I didn't want to visit a dead man—particularly one who had been my best friend—I guess I knew it was inescapable from the moment Holster departed and was followed by Blue Dog and Sandy. Otherwise, I would need to spend years evading their questions of why I hadn't joined them that night.

When I got to Wayne's Feed, I departed the furrow and trudged up the ridge through the thigh-deep white billows. My legs cut through the powder fairly easily, but my feet crunched when they hit the day-old snow beneath the fresh cover. Every fourth step or so, one of my boots broke through the crust and I had to maneuver my way out with a forward lunge. The snow still poured down hard, which gave the landscape an eerie, dreamlike feel. I could not make out any houses strung up the ridge until I was fifty yards from Larkspur's; if not for the beckoning of his yellow, rectangular windows, I'm not sure I could have seen it through the thick veil. When I got within ten yards, my pant legs were damp and snow had made its way into my boots, despite the fact that they were pretty well-sealed. I could hear the music of "Dead Flowers" by the Stones calling from his little three-room cabin.

Next I heard laughter, and then muffled voices. I walked across the porch and in the door to be hit with loud chatter and the sight of a dozen or more of Larkspur's friends and acquaintances drinking his whiskey, a few singing along with the words *"you can send me dead flowers every morning."*

Holster stumbled to greet me, holding a Jack Daniel's bottle by the neck. His face was bright pink and his cheeks were slick with tears. He never could hold his liquor, and it had become worse in recent years when his liver seemed no longer able to absorb or process as quickly.

"Look at him, just look at him," he pleaded, thumping me on the chest with the palm of his left hand while casting his right arm back to indicate Larkspur's position on the floor. "He used to be the life of the party, and now, and now, look at him, look at him. . . ."

There was so much wrong with both his statement and his tone—which seemed to imply that Larkspur was intentionally being a party pooper—that I couldn't summon a response. So, I said nothing. I glanced at the back of Larkspur's head, thrown against the chair arm like he had recoiled to sneeze. A stalk of his blond hair stood straight up. For the time my eyes were in that direction, I kept them locked on the hair. I didn't want to look any farther down. That same chill that had passed through me at the bar ripped once more through my system.

Molly Quinn sat facing him cross-legged. She was chattering intently at his corpse, singing *"And I won't forget to put roses on your grave."*

I could not remember where Molly had come from—Ohio? Wisconsin? Indiana? Somewhere in the Midwest. Blond with marble-blue eyes, she was a bit of a New Ager, did enough high-priced facials, back massages, and fortune-telling for the tourists in the summer to hold her through the winter months.

Everyone in town had dropped out or was hiding out in one way or another. Unless a person volunteered his or her past, it was rude to ask. Who knew what they might be running from or trying to forget? (It was the way I heard it was in prison; no one ever asked the other cons what they were in for.) In fact, it had taken me years to learn many of their real names. Most people had adopted nicknames or aliases, variations on their real names or made-up to fit their personalities or sound American Indian (a few actually were Indian; we were just a few miles from the Crow Reservation). I knew that Holster (from whom I had learned prison etiquette) had served time for robbing banks and his first name was really Ted. Though I had known him for over fifteen years, I don't think I ever heard his last name. I suppose I could find out without too much trouble if it became urgent; I doubted it ever would. He was a bit of a goof who got caught during his third robbery for forgetting his plastic gun with his fingerprints at the scene. I had known Larkspur for over a year when I learned his real name was Rick Larster because one of his sisters passed through town. That was when we still had the same vague idea that, for us, dropping out was only temporary, that we could take a break from time—that someday when we were ready, we could just slip back in our middle-class lives.

I questioned my suggestion not to move him. By leaving him prone, I imagined we were creating more trouble for ourselves when we had to drag him out the next day after rigor mortis had taken full effect. Too late now. Surely over three hours had passed. How long, I wondered, did rigor last? How long until the body started to decompose? At least he was a good distance from the flickering fireplace.

"It's up to us now, buddy, up to us to be the lives of the party," said Holster, draping a loose limb around my neck and hanging on.

I shivered. Thinking that anything was up to me was not what I wanted to hear.

The door opened again and Goose and Flying Hawk, both in their mid-thirties, neither in town for more than three or four years, came sauntering inside. Still amateurs. Despite the living-off-the-land act he put on, Flying Hawk was the son of a wealthy politician from Connecticut. I knew for a fact that he lived off a trust fund, but it wasn't my business to call him on his little ruse. Goose was running from the law—for what, I didn't know—though he and Holster seemed less ashamed of their pasts than Flying Hawk was of his privileged one. Like I said, we all had something to hide.

"Aren't you going to pay your respects?" Holster asked me.

There was nothing I wanted to do less. I had seen my share of dead men. Corky, a pal who had lived in Doe Ridge until the mid-1990s, had spun off the road and been killed on a bike trip we took down the Baja coast. At first we had just thought he had hit his head and was resting on the side of the road. After it became clear he wasn't catching his breath, it took a long time to figure out how to strap him to Larkspur's back and tie his arms around his waist so we could ride him back to the States. At customs, they didn't even notice we had a dead man on the back of a bike. Of course, Corky, like Larkspur, was fair and blond, and the accident took place before 9/11, when they didn't pay a lot of attention to white men going north. We never went back for the bike. The road was desolate; we figured it would be gone or stripped by the time we could return.

Wolf had drowned on a fishing trip. I had helped drag him out of the icy water. I could still remember the cold, rubbery feel of his flesh.

Red Burns had said he was going to chop down that gnarled pine that blocked his view (he lived another quarter mile above Larkspur's place) if it was the last thing he did—and it was; he had a stroke. I had seen more than one overdose and car crash, and now, strange and premature as it seems, a few guys close to my age have dropped off of heart attacks without much warning.

The worst death I witnessed was that of John Jones. We were camping and climbing our way up the mountain when a little late-season snow turned into a blizzard and we were lost in boundless snow glare for two days. He walked off a cliff. Later, the coroner's office said he had never seen it coming. It was snow blindness, or as it read in the autopsy report, *niphablepsia*. The sun shining through the bright white had actually burned off the surfaces of his corneas. Later still, we found out that his name was really Olin Salander and he had left a wife and three children in Minnesota. I had looked up niphablepsia and learned it referred to psychic blindness as often as it did to the actual physical condition caused by the snow.

"Come on, talk to our friend," said Holster, a heavy weight on my side, dragging me toward Larkspur as if he was a walking anchor. I twirled around, freeing myself of his grasp, and he slid—clutching, trying to hold on—down my side to land on all fours. He didn't even bother to react to the way I had spurned him; instead, he crawled to a corner. It looked like he was on the verge of tears but later I heard him snoring.

~

As the night wore on, it seemed as if all but a dozen or so of the people in town over the age of eighteen had managed to fight the blizzard to cram into Larkspur's cabin. The place was just one long room with a kitchen at the far end, a fireplace in the middle, and a bedroom and bath off to the south side. Out of the corner of one eye, I could see his bedroom crowded with people, at least four or five sitting in a sinking circle on his bed. Out of the corner of the other eye, I caught glimpses of Larkspur's head, his green-flannel-clad right arm flung to the right. Larkspur had had clear-green eyes, and that shirt had always brought out their radiance. I hoped Sandy had thought to close his eyes.

I never stopped drinking that night, but I don't think I ever really got drunk. I existed more in fugue state, drifting from one desultory conversation to another, anecdotes about Larkspur (I smiled and nodded but noted that none of them really captured his essence), tales of traveling through the snow to reach his cabin, talk of how much Larkspur would have enjoyed his going-away party (a view I doubted but didn't correct), and drunken rambling. As much as I tried not to look, Larkspur was almost always in my peripheral vision. I noticed that almost everyone spent some time with him; a few of the women just sat with him, weeping. I looked at the objects he owned—a few lamps, rag rugs, and handmade tables; all the chairs except the armchair he leaned against were wooden—scattered around his place and wondered what would happen to them. A few of them, like the lampshade hand-painted with a cowboy rodeo scene, the framed arrow-heads, and the mounted head of a trout had seemed unique treasures. Now, they looked like just so much junk. It was as if the moment that his spirit had departed his body, the objects he owned had lost their sacred-ness. I imagined little spirits "passing" from the tangible entities. I winced at the thought of the junk packed into my own place, stuff I believed I might need some day but clearly never would. His sisters wouldn't want his stuff anymore than my brother would want mine. I didn't think his parents were alive, but I couldn't remember him saying they had died. Except for the stereo, I doubted there was anything of much more value than Holster's snipped ponytail. Larkspur wasn't one for keepsakes. I was surprised he had photos, the ones spread between his legs. I remembered he had a camera from time to time, but I don't recall ever being shown any prints.

When his bed cleared of all but two people, I drifted into the room and fell onto the strip of available space. I had a few waking dreams in which Larkspur was ambulatory. He came in and sat next to me and said, "We better not waste any more time." I remembered my father screaming at me that I was wasting time, and then I remembered how he had been forced into early retirement and had actually molded a spot into his favor-ite armchair that faced the television in the den where my brother and I had played Chutes and Ladders and, later, Monopoly. I started to mumble something about him being the one wasting time when he morphed back into Larkspur. So I tried to tell him about my father, but his form turned into Rainbow Twiller, a beautiful young woman in her teens or early twen-ties with rippling, red hair to her waist, who was really sitting beside me on the bed. I remembered that I had been in love with her once and wondered if Larkspur and my father weren't right, that I shouldn't waste any more time. I took her hand and thought of proposing. She laughed and asked if I was okay, then I remember that it had been her mother, Sunshine, who I had loved, and she had been married and divorced since the long-ago summer we were in love.

"Do you need some coffee?" Rainbow asked.

"What are you doing here?"

"I'm still on break," she said. "The new term doesn't start for another week."

That wasn't what my question had intended. I meant how had she gotten to the place where she had arrived, to being an adult in college? I recalled an image of her, a two- or three-year-old with a mass of unkept pumpkin-colored hair, sitting on Sunshine's lap while Sunshine shucked corn. I had been a few feet away, tossing horseshoes with a few guys. Her boyfriend had just taken off and we had just started up. I wanted to impress her with my agile body and my skill at the game.

"Yes," I said. "Coffee would be good."

In another minute—or it could have been an hour—she was beside me again with a steaming, blue-speckled enamel mug of coffee. I remembered the cup from Sundays on Larkspur's porch and from endless camping trips. I sat up and took a sip. It tasted bitter, sending a jolt through my system. No one else besides the two of us was in the bedroom now, and I could see that only a few people—the professionals—remained in the living room. The darkness had faded to a murky gray that had consumed the comforting light of the lamps. I sipped as she quietly stroked my hair, nothing sexual; it was if I was the child and she was the consoling adult.

"I've got to take off. Are you going to be okay to get home?" she asked. "It is still pretty bad out there, and I didn't see your truck. I've got my mom's; it will cut through anything."

"I'll be fine," I said.

I finished most of the cup, stood—still a bit wobbly—and entered the main room. Larkspur sat by himself, his head still thrown back, though it had rolled a little to the side. In fact, his whole body listed a bit. For the first time since I had been there, I allowed my eyes to fall to his face. His eyes— I was relieved—had been closed. His blond eyelashes rested softly on his bold cheekbones. I pulled on my coat and hat and walked over to his corpse. I squatted beside him for a second. I had nothing to say. I knew he couldn't hear, and I hated Holster's sloppy sentimentality (he still snored in the corner); besides, it seemed right to have a moment of silence with what remained behind of Larkspur. As I was about to stand, I noticed the last photo that had been in his hand; it had slipped from his partially closed fingers to rest, curled, against his thigh. I plucked it up. The yellowing photo was a group shot of Corky who had flown off his bike in Mexico, John Jones who had walked off the cliff in the blizzard, and Larkspur and me, all in a row, our arms draped around each other—the man's version of paper dolls—and big grins on our faces. We stood in front of a pup tent. The shot was taken on that trip up the mountain when John Jones walked off the cliff. It was funny; I didn't remember Corky being with us and couldn't recall who might have taken the photo. Odder still was the fact that all of the men in the photo except me were now dead.

I held the photo pinched between my right thumb and forefinger as I left the cabin, squinting into the bright white. The light behind the thick flurry of snow seemed to ignite the clotted flakes, giving the white a lilac-colored cast. The buildings of the town were no more than purplish-blue forms in the distance. I thought about walking down to the cleared main road, then back up the ridge when I got below my place. Then, I decided just to trudge down the unplowed lane. I wasn't worried about snow blindness; it would take me no more than forty minutes to get home, and if necessary I could walk every inch of town and the surrounded area with or without actual sight.

I moved to clamp the corner of the photo between my teeth while I dug in my pockets for my gloves. As I lifted my hand, an image of myself as a child flashed across the solid white canvas: *I grasped my brother's waist from behind, my legs hooked around his, as we tore down the hill behind our elementary school on an old sled with blades, and then I heard the sound of my mother calling to come in for dinner, though the hill was nowhere near our house.* The memory, buried for at least four decades, appeared so suddenly, so clearly, so viscerally that I could see the yarn of the blue-and-green striped mittens I had worn as a boy and long forgotten. In the second that I claimed and lost the memory, the photo escaped my grasp and flew up into the dense, white pointillism. I jogged forward to catch it, but the wind and the descent of the spiraling snow were too erratic, blowing in so many directions that I was helpless to figure out the photo's trajectory to follow it, and forced to watch as the thin square lifted, dropped, and ascended again to be quickly eaten by a cavity in the white nothingness.

Feast

I am not a judgmental sort. It is not my job. Luke 6:37 *Judge not, and ye shall not be judged; condemn not, and ye shall not be condemned.* That said, I can't say I blamed those who did judge them when they first arrived, which amounts to about everyone in these parts. And who couldn't help but be curious? And gossip. I wasn't opposed to a bit of gossip here and there. Particularly since they moved in right across the road from us, so we had a bird's-eye view. Like I used to tell Oakley, if gossip's my worst sin, I don't think they'll slam the pearly gates when they see me coming.

Now I'm not so sure.

The first time I saw Echo, she looked odd, a combination business-woman and hippie—if hippies even exist anymore. That day she wore a tailored suit, but had frizzy, black hair that hung past her shoulders (not curled or straightened). Her two little girls were dressed in what looked like matching feed sacks. They had dark, curly hair; most kids around here are towheads, except the migrant kids who come up with their folks to work the fields during harvest seasons. The husband, Joseph, was not much to look at, tall and pale as a mortician, close to seven feet. Not that Sims down at the funeral home is tall or pale. I mean what one would *expect* a mortician would look like. Joseph had a funny hairstyle I seen on a few TV actors, a little dark shoot combed up in front, stuck in place with spray.

We didn't think the Hobart place would ever sell, too small for a proper farm, Hobart the older selling bits and pieces over the years, and so run-down. For a while, I thought the Clemmens might buy the land and annex it on to their place, hungry as they are to own everything. But even they didn't want it. The windows boarded up, the skinny barn slanting to the left like a tree caught in a never-ending wind. The FOR SALE sign had blown partway out of the frame so you couldn't read the words anymore—though what else would it say?

Then, up they show in a car barely large enough to hold the four of them, as bright-orange and round as a giant Florida tangerine, a car that I would later learn plugs in at night! I saw their arrival from my front porch, so I walked up that long, loopy driveway to see if they were lost or needed anything. Those little girls were running round and round the outside of the barn; the mortician was walking back and forth on the saggy front porch; and Echo was clipping circles in the dust between the house and the barn—high heels as tall and thin as knitting needles—talking into a cell phone she held up to her ear under a sheath of that hair. All their running and circling, like a bunch of clocks gone haywire.

None of them seemed to notice me.

"Can I help you?" I called ahead so as not to startle them.

The girls kept running and the man kept walking, his head down, like he was deep in thought, but Echo looked up, snapped her phone shut, arched an eyebrow and smiled. She was pretty in a very made-up way, a television announcer–type way.

"May I help you?" she asked.

"I live across the road, wondered if you were lost or something."

"Oh, our new neighbor!" she chirped. Her smile grew wider and brighter, a mouth full of shiny, white teeth, the kind you see on toothpaste commercials. I felt my right hand flutter up to cover my own smile. I wish I had got that gray tooth in the front replaced. We had the money, but I just couldn't get past paying so much for such a small piece of me.

She walked toward me, her hand extended. I might not have noticed that her nail polish matched her lipstick if they both hadn't been as orange as the car. "We just bought the place."

You could have knocked me over from the wind of a butterfly wing. But I give myself credit. I didn't miss a beat. I lowered my hand from my mouth and took her hand. Her hand had a bony look to it but felt strangely soft and cold. She had a firm shake. I stuffed my hand in my apron pocket right after we shook so she wouldn't see my nails. It was going to be a lot of work hiding all the parts of me that needed to be out of sight in her company.

"Welcome. Always glad to have a new neighbor. When you moving in?"

"Soon as we can get the place renovated, probably a month or two. We would like to get inside before midsummer."

I didn't mention that I thought fixing up that place would take more than a month or two. Most people did their own renovations. Glad I didn't since I couldn't have been more wrong. The very next day, two or three crews showed, mostly up from Detroit but they hired some locals too. In less than forty-five days the house was cleaned up, fitted with new windows, painted, and enlarged by a stone addition bigger than the house itself—almost looked like the house was pulling a trailer—and they straightened the barn and painted the siding bright-orange! Put in a big skylight too, right where the loft door used to be. But that wasn't the most of it. On my day taking care of my granddaughter, Linda, June's daughter, when I'm gone from seven a.m. until seven p.m., I come home to find the driveway straight. The curly mess had always been a problem for Hobart hauling equipment. Who would have thought it could be pulled straight in one day, like a dead snake hung from a nail? After dinner, Oakley and I walked across the road to see how they done it. Turns out they just patched the swirls with sod, but you could only see that real close-up.

Echo—she called herself, though I later learned her real name was Ellen—knew how to get things done. Turned out they were both attorneys. Joseph and Echo. They were from out east but wanted to farm. Or "play farm," as some would say. The fruit trees already there, plus some vegetables, a few chickens. Maybe a goat or two. Obviously they had money.

Oakley didn't like the brightly colored barn, an eyesore, he called it. He liked things solid and simple. Most folks I knew did. I'm not judgmental, thought I would wait and see.

"Might be cheerful in the winter," said I. "Judge not, and you will not be judged."

He gave me that look he has. Like I said, I'm not a religious person really. I learned the Bible backward and forward when I was a kid, so the words pop into my head whether I want them or not. But that time, with Oakley, I was being purposeful. No need to bad-mouth people we hadn't really got to know. Oakley could be a bit hardheaded and disapproving. His mother was what the kids call a Bible-thumper, and Oakley—though even less religious than me—still fears her. Never mind that she's been in the ground eight years. He won't retort words of the Bible.

"I'm just glad they're sticking to chickens and an orchard. None of them heritage pigs."

We are pig farmers, a good-sized operation—farrow to finish—family-run, third generation. My family was chicken farmers, looked down on by the pig farmers. We got laughed at on the school bus for being stinky. Folks who don't know farming might think it more couth to raise chickens. But that is not the case. They are less profitable and smell more than pigs. So when Oakley and I tied the knot, people said that I married up.

Oakley is not an unhandsome man. At forty-five years old, his face is probably even more handsome than at twenty—rugged and angular— though his good looks are undercut by his belly, which sticks out over his waistband, solid, like the tin bread basket his mother had, one with the roses stenciled on the curving door. It tickles me that the rest of his body is in perfect proportion except for the belly, his arms and legs as solid as river rock.

My family's chicken farm went bust when daddy died, sold out to the Clemmons. My four brothers headed to Detroit for factory jobs—the two older ones managed to retire before the car business went bust; the other two returned and work for Oakley now. We only keep a few chickens for eggs, a few for fryers. Oakley was twenty when we married and I was eighteen. Had our three kids, one right after another. Got that out of the way so we could relax. My oldest, June-bug, got married at twenty, like her daddy, so I was a grandma before I turned forty. I only babysit that one day a week. That way she only has to pay for day care two days. She only works three long days a week as a hairdresser. Our younger boys left home as soon as they could. Billy went to college and works in Chicago now. Oakley Jr. manages a hardware store in Grand Rapids. Oakley wasn't too happy to take my younger brothers on when they lost their jobs, but he's mighty glad he has them now that it doesn't look like there's going to be a fourth generation running the Wilkenson Pig Farm.

But I am getting too far afield.

Echo was friendly enough that first week they moved in, but declined my invitation for coffee, asked for a rain check. She took the pie and the canned peach preserves when I walked them over, though she didn't invite me in. I took no offense. There was something in her eyes, two things—a brightness and wariness, if both of them can gather together like that in one set of eyes—that made me think she was biding her time until she could trust me. She usually was the one to walk down the drive to collect the mail. The one time I seen her husband walk down to the box, I scurried outside as fast as I could to see if it would be any easier to pry information out of him than out of her.

I expected a refined voice. You could have knocked me over when I realized he had a stutter. By that time, I had already heard he was a lawyer from Patsy at the beauty parlor where June works, who had heard it from the real estate lady, Martha Cooper. How could you say all that legal jargon in court with a stutter? The stutter come out when I asked him if he thought it might rain.

"It da-da-da-doesn't look like it to me."

I tested him with another question.

"Would you like to ride into town with us for church tomorrow?" I focused on his eyes so I would not stare at the little sprout of hair.

"We don't a-a-a-attend church."

I have to admit, it was a kind of double test. I sort of suspected they might not be the churchgoing type, just wanted to know for sure. But it was more than just a test. I would have loved to have everyone piled into our car, forced to talk. I admit I get lonely out here all day. No neighbors. No women to talk to except on Sundays and shopping day. And if they had a been churchgoers, no matter which religion, we could ride together; all of the churches face each other diagonally on the corners of the village green—except the Catholic church. You have to drive over to Clarkston if you're Catholic. I had been brought up in Seventh-day Adventist Church, switched to Baptist when my dad had a fight with the new preacher about raising fryers for eating. At that time we didn't indulge, just sold 'em. Genesis 9:4: *But flesh with the life thereof, which is the blood thereof, shall ye not eat.* The preacher before him didn't mind even if you ate 'em, long as you stuck to moderation and stayed away from pork. But the new guy was holier than thou. He even made us get a new version of the Bible with the wording a bit different, hard to remember what came from which version, everything changed around so much. He didn't last a year, but once we left there was no going back. Daddy had only gone to the Seventh-day Adventist in the first place because of my mom, no point after she passed. The Baptist church wasn't too bad, not like I hear the Southern Baptists are, just a few holy rollers like Oakley's mom, which is why neither of my boys stuck it out past sixteen. Like I said, I know my Bible, but I'm not overly religious; church is just what you do, rounds off the week and makes time to think and talk to folks.

But there I go, straying off subject, repeating myself again.

I can't say for sure when it was my mind changed from thinking about Echo, her stuttering husband, and those two tattered girls in a mildly curious way to them all—particularly Echo—taking up a bigger space in my brain than just about everything else. It was not a pleasant type of thinking. I don't quite remember ever being stuck on a person like that, except maybe Amy, who had been my best friend up through sixth grade. She come from another chicken-farming family, sat with me on the bus and at lunch, played with me and my brothers in the barn on the swing ropes. That all changed in the sixth grade, when on Saturdays girls started biking into town to the drugstore for a milkshake or were dropped at the mall one county over. But in the way of the Seventh-day Adventists, I had to spend Saturdays in church. Amy was a Methodist, could do whatever she wanted on Saturday. I will never forget the noontime I was waiting at our lunch table in the school cafeteria and I seen Amy pay the cashier and leave the line, carrying her tray. She was wearing a plaid jumper, homemade, over a white blouse. I watched the way her eyes never looked in my direction as she carried her tray to the table where the Saturday mall girls sat. I suppose her socializing paid off. Later on, Amy would become the queen of the Michigan Blossomtime Festival, wore a crown and rode a float in the big parade.

And Oakley, of course; my mind had been stuck on Oakley for a time, but the fixation loosened once he gave me my ring.

With Echo, I even changed my evening stroll—my exercise walk—to go west (right into the eye of the setting sun) instead of east, just so I could go up the incline that allowed me to see into their front yard. Mostly Echo and her husband sat on the porch reading or holding long-stemmed glasses that sparkled in the setting sun. The girls chased each other or sat across from each other, dolls in the middle. They were always together—twins, I would later learn, their births made possible by in vitro, what Oakley and I would have called test-tube babies. Not that we had anything against that—being pig farmers, we were used to scientific breeding methods.

If they saw me, I would wave, and they waved back.

Sometimes, after the walk, I would stand behind the block of hollyhocks that grow around my front porch, hoping the bushes hid me, watching. Not very satisfying. I couldn't see much from that distance. Though, the barn glowed a real fiery orange during the sunset.

Once their house went dark for three days running. On the third night after my walk, I stopped right in the middle of the road, staring at their place, and remembered a time—buried so deep in my head that I had forgotten it until that moment—when I had walked the three miles to Amy's farm, pretending I was casually strolling past, hoping she would see me and come rushing out.

During that three-day stretch of darkness, I was all cranky, worried that maybe they had gotten bored and were moving. I couldn't sleep from thinking about them. When they got home—shooting up the driveway in their orange thingamajig—I felt all my bones sag in relief. Not that it made no never mind. They continued to keep to themselves. New information on them was slow in coming even though I found ways to bring them into about every conversation I had at the grocery store or church. It reminded me of back before Oakley gave me the ring. That had not been a pleasant feeling either, trying to get his name in every other word in every conversation, scribbling his name on my notepaper instead of listening in class, but at least it had made some sense and had a natural end to it.

I wasn't quite sure what was happening to me. I even snapped at Oakley when he called Joseph a weirdo. And the day Echo come to borrow some eggs, I was beside myself.

"How much can I pay you?" she asked.

"No need. I'm sure I'll ask you for something one day." I couldn't imagine what.

"But it's your business."

"No, we're pig farmers."

After I put together a basket, she could hardly decline my offer of a cup of coffee. I took her into the parlor. A bit silly and old-fashioned having a parlor these days, but Oakley's mother had it before me and her mother-in-law before that. When our kids were little, Oakley built a family room onto the back of the house. Now we even have a wide-screen television (pig farming has been good to us) and all new furniture, except for in the parlor. Usually that's where we take important visitors like the preacher. It seemed fitting that I take Echo there, where the family antiques and heirlooms were kept, lace curtains instead of blinds or drapes. I made the right choice.

"What exquisite antiques!"

"Family heirlooms," I said, wondering if I had ever spoken the word exquisite aloud.

She took the big chair where Oakley's grandfather had carved the back up like it was a tree trunk, all knotty, with hand-whittled birds and squirrels posed along the side rails, a squirrel stretched out on each arm, and a pile of acorns at the top. The chair always fascinated my granddaughter, Linda. I sometimes had to pry her out of it to get her back in the television room where there was nothing to break except the television and it was up on the wall (I hope Linda hasn't inherited that thing I have where sometimes her mind gets stuck on things). Echo and I had been sitting there two minutes when I felt the silence. Here was my opportunity to strike up a conversation and I couldn't think of a word. I didn't want to just make small talk—and given she didn't know anyone, we couldn't gossip.

"Once I have some time, I hope to do a little antiquing," said Echo.

"I can show you the best places," I said, immediately regretting it because there were no best places. The only antique stores I knew were really junk stores, except for the place in Clarkston so overpriced that only a fool would shop there. "I never really have time myself, but I love the *Antiques Roadshow.*"

I wanted to show her that I wasn't a hick. I might have lived in the same little Michigan farm town my entire life, but I had been (unlike many of my neighbors) to Detroit and Chicago.

I don't know whether it was my mention of that particular show or just her pleasure in looking at my antiques, but somehow what we were saying turned into a real conversation, more of one than I had had with anyone in a long time. We talked about what we liked about old things and how quiet it was at night on Hobart Road. We talked about the hollyhocks in my front yard—not about how they were doing that year, but what it was about hollyhocks that made them so interesting-looking.

"They're so tall, they look like flower walls—or as if real wallpaper has bloomed and come to life," said Echo. For a moment I wondered if she was on to me, spying from behind them, but we were on to another subject too quickly.

"Just think of the imagination it would take to carve this chair," she said, looking around and behind her. "I once wanted to be a sculptor."

Before she went into law, she had studied art. She loved beautiful things, but her father thought law was more practical. She snickered when she said this, but it didn't really change the odd beauty of her face. The right eye appeared slightly larger than the left. Both were as big, shiny, and mahogany-colored as buckeyes; it was just that the lid drooped on the left one and the skin below seemed to be sliding up. Like one eye was squinting and the other was staring. The bridge of her nose was so long and narrow that it was like an invisible thumb and forefinger were pinching it together. And her lips were plump, the way I know television actresses like them these days. Except for the puppet lines around her mouth, she didn't have a single wrinkle. But the most amazing thing was her lipstick, which stayed deep and brilliant-orange no matter how much she talked and sipped coffee. I could barely get my lipstick to last from the mirror inside our front door to the church vestibule. Her crinkly hair was a dark black, but somehow seemed to have hints of the same orange of her lips, yet when I tried to locate the lighter hair strands, they weren't to be found. They were just hidden somewhere in that mass of frizz.

She did estate planning for wealthy folks in New York. With the Internet, she only needed to go back two or three times a month. She didn't go to church because she was Jewish! (The first Jewish person I knew more than just in passing.) Numbers 6:27: *And they will put my name on the Israelites, and I will bless them.* Echo had growed tired of the bustle of New York, wanted more privacy. I didn't mention that it didn't matter whether there were folks around for miles or not—everyone here knew everyone's business. (We all already assumed she was from New York since Rich, the mailman, said most of her correspondence came from there. He said the word *Esquire* by their names meant they were lawyers.)

We talked for a long time. The words flowed, not too fast or too slow. Just natural. Like we had known each other for a long time. The only awkward moment came when we discovered we were the exact same age. Neither of us said it, but we both must have been wondering how I could be a grandmother and so plain and old-looking, and her with little kids and so young-looking. But the pause didn't last long.

I don't know that we would have stopped talking if the back screen door hadn't slapped when Oakley came in from his day.

"What you doing in here?" he asked as he entered the parlor. His question irritated me—I wanted Echo to think I sat in the parlor all the time. But Echo didn't seem to hear him; she was looking at her watch.

"OhmyGod," she said in a rush, all crammed together like one word. "Look at the time. I'm expecting someone; I've got to get home."

She looked at the basket of eggs sitting on the small round table in the corner.

"Oh no. They've been sitting out," she said. "They've probably gone bad."

"Eggs?" I asked. "If it's not a hot spell, they can sit out all day."

"Really? They don't need to be refrigerated?"

I laughed, then Oakley laughed, then we all laughed. Ha, ha, ha, ha.

"I guess I really am a city slicker," she said. I liked that she was a good sport.

As she lifted the basket, she tapped the table with the rounded knuckles of her right hand, and said, "You should take good care of this. I think it's a Stickley. Could be valuable."

Odd, of all the pieces in the room it was the plainest.

After she left, it was too late for the meatloaf I had planned, so I made hamburgers from the defrosted beef. Over dinner, I was careful what I told Oakley about Echo. I wanted the information I had learned about her to be just mine for a while longer. I felt so full of life, bursting, that I didn't wash the dishes after eating before I went out for my walk. I was young, I thought, other folks my age had young children, wore orange lipstick, and flew to New York City regular. I raced up the hill and turned to look down on the Hobart place. There was a black convertible in the driveway. A man in blue jeans and a black T-shirt stood in a little triangle with Echo and Joseph. He had shoe-polish dark hair, was muscular, shorter than Joseph, maybe shorter than me. The girls crouched in the dirt by the car in front of what looked like a new kitten. After a minute, Joseph and the girls and the kitten got into the orange car and took off down the straight driveway and turned away from town, toward the Dairy Queen. Echo and the visitor climbed up the porch steps into the house. It looked like they were holding hands, though I couldn't really tell from my vantage point.

I watched the sunset, pink and blue, behind the orange barn before returning home.

"How was your walk?" asked Oakley. He sat in front of the widescreen watching a show on the commodities market.

"The sunset was exquisite."

~

The next day, I floated through my chores until I seen Sally Jacobs at Mike's Market, our silver carts going in opposite directions, in the wide frozen foods aisle. Sally is the church secretary, goes in four days a week. I doubted there was enough work for four days, but she liked the prestige and hearing the gossip. I known her in high school when the last thing one would expect her to become was a church secretary. Sally veered the front end of her cart in beside mine in a way that suggested I pause, and looked at me with her little pink rabbit eyes. You would have thought she was an albino if she hadn't informed everyone from grade school on that she had been tested by an out-of-town doctor and he had certified her normal. When we were younger, both her hair and skin were white as the classroom chalk, her faint purple veins a shadowy lattice right beneath the skin. Everyone teased her, so I guess it was no surprise that she became what was called *loose* in high school. By the end of high school, I was in the Baptist church, not an outcast like the others who went to church on Saturday. I wasn't what one would call in with the popular crowd but friendly enough to hear the stories. Didn't know how her fragile skin could hold all the makeup she shoveled on. But I have to admit, there was an odd, delicate beauty to the way she looked. Got pregnant our senior year by Pastor John's son, married him, and did a complete turnaround. No one more pious, and a good thing too, since her looks completely drained out of her, like she had no blood left after having four children. Now her hair was the dull, translucent white of boiling spaghetti noodles. It was almost like a see-through ghost stood there in front of me by the frozen vegetable freezer case.

"So, what did you find out about your new neighbor's religious affiliation?" she asked.

"Must worship in New York. She goes there all the time."

"Maybe you could bring her with you some Sunday, see if she likes First Baptist. I, for one, would like to meet her." I felt Sally goading me.

"Well, I'm not sure I'll get a chance to introduce you 'til our annual pig roast come September."

Don't know why I didn't come right out and tell her that Echo was Jewish. That would have been gold in the world of gossip. Though, the mention of New York could be a giveaway for some. Of course there's them that's prejudice around here, but for the most part, us at the Baptist church had a healthy respect for the Israelites. More so than the Catholics, who looked to the pope. If you were a believer, you knew the Jews would do a turnaround in the end. I guess I didn't tell Sally because she was a gossip, not like me, more of the mean kind, the kind who had to get back at folks. I never was like that. Even when Amy became Blossomtime Queen, I never mentioned any of the bad stuff I knew about her childhood or her unkindness to me. I pushed it out of mind, didn't even think about it.

"Echo, I hear that's a made-up name," said Sally. "You have to wonder about them that would change the name that God gave 'em."

"I think it more likely that her parents was the ones that gave it. When you think of it, I'm surprised so many folks stick with what their parents call them."

"Honor thy father and mother," said Sally.

"*Romans 12:2: And be not conformed to this world, but be ye transformed by the renewing of your mind*," I said and smiled, before I thought twice. And then even worse, I added, "Well, I would love to hang around and trade Bible verses with you, but I've got places to go, people to see!"

The look on her face! It would have been comical if not for the fact that I knew I had just created a dangerous enemy. She had the ear of everyone who walked into the preacher's office. The feeling of pure joy I had been experiencing ever since my conversation with Echo began to dissolve at the checkout line and had reached near rock bottom by the time I loaded the groceries in the truck. I didn't feel like myself the next few days, moping around the house. I seen the orange car and the black car come and go, but didn't see Echo, even on my nightly walks.

I was hanging the sheets out to dry—of course, we have a washer and dryer, but sometimes the smell of the breeze in them when we go to sleep at night is soothing—a wooden clothespin in my mouth, when I heard Echo call my name.

"Val!"

I turned to see her and the short, muscular man standing on edge of the gravel drive. The clothespin dropped from my lower lip, tumbled down my chest to the ground, and I laughed. They laughed too. We all stood there laughing at nothing, like a couple of school kids.

"Valerie, this is Harry. He's here from New York for a few weeks."

"Hello, Harry," I said, and we shook hands. If Echo was exotic in her own way, Harry was movie-star handsome in the face, with the same deep, buckeye brown eyes as her. Dark hair, an aquiline nose. The whitest teeth I had ever seen in real life outside of Echo's; probably her brother. Yet he wasn't off-putting the way I would expect someone with his looks to be.

"The peaches are so ripe that they're all falling off our trees," said Echo. "I don't know what to do with them—we can't eat them all. Then I remembered those amazing peach preserves you brought me when we moved in and I was wondering"—she looked at Harry for support—"we were wondering if you might have time to show us how to make jam?"

I must have looked dumbfounded because Harry piped in, "We would compensate you, of course, pay you."

"No need for that," I said. "Just let me keep a few jars. I do my canning and jam-making with peaches from the market when they go on half-price. Your peaches would be enough compensation. Just help me get the extra jars out of the basement—do you want to work at my place or yours?"

I had a ton of errands and chores to do, what with moping around I had fallen behind, but I didn't hesitate for a second. Glad I didn't. When I think back, I can't remember an afternoon in the last ten years when I had more fun. Oakley was meeting with a restaurant owner out west at a Lake Michigan resort who wanted to become farm-to-table. Joseph had taken Echo's girls into Chicago for the last weekend trip before school started. Echo was excited that the girls would be taking a yellow school bus to the elementary school, though she thought she might have to send them away once they reached junior high. She wasn't sure about the local high school.

"I don't blame you one bit," I said. "What with meth labs starting up and all. Our high school isn't safe as when I was there."

We took a basket of jars over to Echo's place. We harvested all the ripe peaches that were still hanging. Harry stopped to juggle when he come across three or more that were firm enough, Echo and I both laughing, particularly when he juggled at the same time he walked along the unwound garden hose sprawled flat in the grass, like he was a high-wire acrobat.

Echo's kitchen looked like something out of a magazine—marble counters, fancy fixtures—including the fact that she had no supplies or machines on the counters besides a food processor and coffee machine, beneath hanging copper pots. Harry ran me home in his convertible three times to get stuff—my canning rack, canning bath, a sack of sugar, and the pectin—I tried to decline the ride, seemed silly, but he insisted and I must say I felt like a movie star, him racing me up and down the drive with the top down. The only thing Echo had that I didn't was limes, which is the secret to the best preserves.

"For gin and tonics," she said, and spit out a little laughter—she had a way of doing that when she come to a punch line or said something that sounded absurd.

"Speaking of which, I could use one right now, with all this steam," said Harry once everything started boiling. "Girls, want me to mix you up some?"

Drinking is generally frowned upon in the Baptist church, but Oakley and my brothers were known to have a couple beers when watching football. And a lot of folks drank beer or hard cider at our pig roast. Oakley and I usually had champagne on New Year's and our anniversary. I had had a few mixed drinks when we were dating and went into Chicago, but that was it.

"*Luke 5:38: But new wine must be put into new bottles; and both are preserved,*" said I before I had a chance to think.

"Wha . . .?" asked Harry. "Are you quoting the Bible?"

He sounded impressed, so I rattled off a few more Bible quotations about wine. All the positive ones that come to mind.

"No way, no how," he said, as he handed me a heavy glass with a wedge of lime. "You're like a biblical scholar or something."

I took a sip. It tasted a little like 7 Up. Refreshing in the steamy kitchen. I took another longer swallow and felt the liquor enter my veins.

We made a mess that afternoon, but talked as easily as Echo and I had in my parlor, laughing, getting bits of peach meat in our hair and on our faces. Turned out Harry was an artist, and he decided to save the peach pits for a project. That's why they had cut the skylight in the barn, so he would have a place to work when he visited. I couldn't imagine what type of art would need peach pits. The women's auxiliary down at the church sometimes made dolls out of corn stalks, liked to bead, and constructed decorative piggy banks and birdhouses out of Clorox bottles, but I was pretty certain Harry wasn't talking about that sort of thing.

"What kind of art uses peach pits?"

"Once I finish the assemblage, I'll take a photo for you," said Harry.

Time got away from me. We were filling the last of the jars when we heard a knock on the door. Harry went to answer it and I heard Oakley ask, "Is my wife—Val—here?"

At the sound of his voice, I almost sobered up. Almost. I gathered my things, that what I could carry, and went out to meet Oakley in the front hall, where he held open the front door for me. I stumbled on the bottom step of the porch, then swayed a bit, drunk with both gin and the magic of the afternoon.

"Are you drunk?" asked Oakley. He sounded more surprised than angry.

"We were putting away peaches," I said as if that were a reasonable reply.

Oakley made canned soup and toast for us for dinner. It was probably only the third time he had cooked anything for us besides eggs on a Sunday morning. The next day was my day to babysit Linda. I had never known a headache could be so splitting, my stomach roiling the entire time. Isaiah 24:9: *Strong drink shall be bitter to them that drink it.* Twelve hours of chasing after a four-year-old sure proved that verse to be more than just a Bible story.

~

I swore never to drink again—except maybe on New Year's or at Linda's wedding—but once the headache was gone, the hangover was like childbirth, hard to remember in its intensity. In the future, when I visited Echo in the late afternoon, during what she and Joseph and Harry called "cocktail hour," I sipped in moderation and never had a second G&T (that's what they called them). We usually sat on the porch and watched the girls play in the yard. They liked to dress up the new kitten that Harry gave them in doll clothes. I always made it a point to get home twenty minutes before Oakley to get dinner started.

Echo talked about me going to New York with her some weekend. Once when she came back she brought with her a tube of that special kind of lipstick she wore, only pinker for my "fair skin." When I wore it to church, the color stayed on until well after the social hour. When I told them about the pig roast, Joseph laughed.

"Good welcome for your new Jewish neighbors," he said.

"What's funny?" I wanted to know.

"As Jews, we aren't supposed to eat pork," said Joseph. Once he got to know a person, he stopped stuttering. And he told me stuttering made little difference in his practice; he wasn't a litigator (I looked that up when I got home). "I'm the only one of us who observed growing up. I don't refrain anymore, but I must say seeing pigs roasting could set me back."

He smiled to show me he was only kidding.

As a Seventh-day Adventist, I hadn't been able to eat pork either. It was funny; we had more in common than anyone would guess.

I began to think of the Labor Day weekend pig roast as Echo's welcoming party. I figured that someone would pry it out of her that she was Jewish at the party. I was proud that I had held my tongue about that, and looked forward to when a body asked me if I had known, telling them that, why yes, of course—what difference did it make?

Oakley always roasted three pigs; more than half the county came. No one paid much mind who drank or what anyone did. We always had it on a Friday night so nobody would be tired for church on Sunday. I didn't see Echo for the two days beforehand since I was so busy making potato salad and pies. I was as nervous as a chicken with my head cut off—which I can testify is a mighty scary sight—the week before the party. Couldn't sleep the night before. Never could, but this year in particular, my mind was like a wasp in a glass jar.

The day of the party, June and Linda got there midafternoon so June-bug could help me set up. Five p.m. sharp, the cars and pickups started arriving. The pigs had already been on the spit for hours. Oakley and my brothers had the horseshoes set up and the net for volleyball. I was setting out the side dishes and bags of chips when I seen Echo and Joseph coming across the road with their two girls. You could have knocked me over with the breeze from a butterfly's wing not to see Harry. I had gotten used to them as a unit.

"Where's Harry?" I called as I walked down the drive to greet them.

"He had to go to New York at the la-la-last minute. A big commission," said Joseph. I guess the prospect of meeting new people had set Joseph's stutter in motion.

Echo gave me a glum look and shrugged. I gave her daughters three dollars each to keep an eye on Linda. June-bug was watching her too, but it made the girls feel grown-up. They were a hard two girls to get to know, always so taken with each other that they didn't pay no mind to others, but I had come to care for them more than I usually did for other people's children. By six, our yard was packed from the house to the barn and splitting its seams in between. Babies. Old folks. Church folks, farmers, and townsfolk—the folks from the shops and the PO. It was only every now and then I caught a glimpse of Echo, and I was happy to see her in conversation. I smiled to myself when I seen Sally Jacobs had Echo backed up to the chicken coop fence. I would have loved to be a fly on the fence post.

I was so busy fetching and refilling that I didn't get a chance to talk to Echo until after the pigs were eaten. We each took a piece of pie and one of them low-slung lawn chairs and drug them up by the big bonfire in front of the pit, next to the girls—Linda's and Echo's—all roasting marshmallows. It warmed my heart that they were getting along. In the chairs, Echo and I were down so low that our knees were up at our chests. When the girls finished, all sticky messes, Joseph took their two home, and June-bug took Linda in to bed. They always spent the night after the pig roast.

"Sorry Harry couldn't make it," I said, sweeping the side of the plastic fork across my paper plate—printed with a pig face for the occasion—to collect the last of my fat slice of cherry pie. On top of my six pies, folks had brought another dozen or so, and more than one of them had a cherry orchard. The roast was always a feast.

"Make that double for me," said Echo. "I'm so depressed."

"Don't think of it that way—you're lucky," I said. "To be so close to your brother."

Echo turned and looked at me. The way the firelight hit her face made her brows exaggerated, like steep tents over her mahogany eyes.

"You thought Harry was my brother?"

"What else would he be—your cousin?"

She looked away as if she was considering something, then back at me, the yellow-orange flickers of the fire dancing on her face, the pitched appearance of the eyebrows lit from below.

"Val, can you keep a secret?"

I paused before I said yes.

"Of course." I lowered my voice.

"Harry is my second husband."

"Wait, you and Joseph are divorced?"

"No, we're polygamous."

I knew the word, of course, there are plenty of examples in the Bible, and I had seen some television programs about Mormons. Still, my mind couldn't quite hook into what she said. Jacob had four wives, but what she was saying made no sense. There were never any other women around her house, then I realized what she meant—second husband—and I shrieked. Echo put her hand on my arm to silence me. It didn't matter; too much music and chatter for anyone to notice.

"You mean . . .?"

She nodded. "Yes, I'm married to them both. Not legally of course, but spiritually. The three of us had a ceremony. You don't hate me, do you? A few friends in New York know about our arrangement. I hadn't planned to tell anyone out here, but we've become so close. I just couldn't have you thinking Harry was my brother."

"But you two look so much alike, your eyes—so dark."

She laughed, that popping sound she made when giving the punch line. "We're both Jewish; there are a lot of people who look somewhat like us in New York. *My tribe.* All of you in Michigan with your sandy hair and fair skin look related to me."

Then I laughed, and we were both laughing like that day in the kitchen, laughing so hard that my gut hurt, laughing so hard that I found myself gasping. When our hilarity finally died down, I told her, "It's okay to tell me, but I wouldn't tell anyone else round here if I was you."

"No, no, I know," she said. "I never even intended to tell you."

We were quiet for a while, a nice quiet, like two friends with a secret, each lost in her thoughts. I was surprised to realize that I had never really had a friend since Amy. Neighbors, ladies in the congregation, people who stopped by for coffee to catch up when out this way, but not a friend who shared a secret (gossip is not the same—that's about others, not one's self), not a person who wanted to go with me to New York or brought me a gift for no reason. It was a warm feeling, mixed with the less warm feeling of knowing she had two husbands. Did she have sex with them both? Or did she stop having sex with Joseph when she started having sex with Harry? Did all three of them have sex together? I admit, despite my feeling of happiness, the whole situation didn't sit totally perfect with me. I wasn't used to having a feeling of happiness and a feeling of uneasiness mingled together. I would get used to it, I figured. Love was love. Our church was against gay marriage, but privately, Oakley and I had said to each other that what did we care if two men or two women loved each other? Luke 6:37: *Judge not, and ye shall not be judged; condemn not, and ye shall not be condemned; forgive, and you will be forgiven.* It might have been my favorite verse.

After the party, we didn't get everything cleaned up until late, my mind churning the whole time. It was almost sunrise by the time Oakley and I flopped down on the bed, the room dark except for a hint of pink at the horizon out the window. I was about to turn to the wall and try to sleep, but then—almost without realizing what I was doing, in a blurry kind of way—I pulled my nightgown over my head, my panties down off my ankles, and slid in the other direction on top of Oakley.

"Whoa," he said, drawing back his face to look me in the eye. "It's practically morning. June-bug's family is sleeping downstairs."

Despite himself, his thing swelled, and I slid it inside me. Sex took on a power I had never felt before. I slithered around in circles on top of him like a snake, playing with the warm bulk inside me, moving it around like I would a lollipop in my mouth, feeling my lower regions opening, getting all moist, bubbly. Oakley grew more than usual; his hardness rubbing against my velvety insides caused needles of painful pleasure to shoot up from my groin until I threw back my head and howled, actually howled like a banshee. He clamped his hand over my mouth, which made it start all over again inside me, only more forceful, like a giant bubble, all pain and pleasure until it burst and sent tingles all the way to the tips of my toes.

The next morning, we were so embarrassed we couldn't look each other in the eye.

~

The week after the roast was confusing. Up and down. Up and down. I loved Echo. I distrusted her. I trusted her. How could love be wrong? But surely being with two men was wrong? Though I didn't consider myself religious in the sense of most folks at First Baptist, I had been brought up on it. Since I knew the Bible better than most, I couldn't just push it aside. Believe 'em or not, those words get inside you.

Yet, for almost everything said in the Bible, you could find the opposite said as well. And what wasn't in the first Bible I learned from was in the second or the one when we changed to the Baptist church.

Corinthians 13:48: *Love does not insist on its own way; it is not irritable or resentful; it does not rejoice at wrongdoing, but rejoices with truth. Love bears all things, believes all things, hopes all things, endures all things. Love never ends. As for prophecies, they will pass away; as for tongues, they will cease.*

I skipped church that Sunday and Echo and I went for a long walk. She had on a pair of bright-orange sneakers that we watched flash against the gravel while we walked. She told me more about how it had come to be, her with both men. Harry had another girlfriend in New York, but she was casual. Echo wasn't looking for men, but sometimes she did sleep with other men. Joseph and Harry knew. But they, the three of them, were in a committed relationship.

I thought about how she always had an interesting comment about the things we passed, made me think of them in new ways, the way she had months earlier when we talked about the hollyhocks. The trees along the crest of a distant hill like the scales on the spine of a giant dinosaur, bundled hay like giant shredded wheat, branches on a certain tree like the veins in Harry's hand. Everything was like something else. She didn't really interrupt our conversation to point them out, just said, "Oh, isn't that like . . ." and kept on talking. I figured it was an artist's eye. She said that was one of the reasons she had first been drawn to Harry, a friend of a client. She missed the art world.

"I know you need time to process all of this," she said.

~

I was excited to see Harry shoot up the drive the next Saturday morning. He rented a different car each trip, convertibles in the warm weather, and drove out from the Detroit airport. He didn't have a car in New York.

My forty-fourth birthday was the next day and we were having a little party, just family, in the late afternoon, after church. Since my birthday always falls so soon after the roast, we tend to keep it small. My brothers who worked the farm were coming. June-bug and her family. Sometimes one or both of my sons came out; not this year. They hadn't been in for the pig roast either. Seems like they were getting on with their lives. That used to bother me, but not so much anymore. People should live their lives the way they wanted, not as their parents had. I waited until after dinner on Saturday to walk over with the invite for Echo and her tribe. I wanted to ask her at the last minute, so it would be more casual, not like I was fishing for a present.

The inside door stood open. I could hear them laughing inside. I felt a smile spread across my face. My whole insides warmed up. I paused for a minute in front of the screen to listen but as what they were saying come into clarity, I felt my cheeks begin to burn. I heard Joseph first.

"How about this: 'Ecclesiastes 4: *If one falls down, his friend can pick him up*'?"

"That's stupid," said Echo.

Then Harry spoke.

"John 15:12: *That someone lays down his life for his friends.*"

"A bit dramatic, don't you think?" said Echo, followed by her little spitting burst of laughter. Then they was all laughing. "Wait, wait, listen to this . . ."

I didn't hear the rest because I ran back down the steps, quietly as I could. My heart pumped as I raced down the drive. They was making fun of me! I was a fool, such a fool. I tried to behave normally when I come in the door, but Oakley could tell something was wrong. I claimed a headache, went into our room, and lay down on the bed, hoping to calm my thumping heart. I crossed my arms over my chest, both hands stacked, pressing my heart, watching the light fade out the bedroom window.

I come out later when the shows came on, so we could just sit and watch without talking.

"I saw Joseph today in town," said Oakley during a commercial break. "They're excited about your birthday."

"You invited them?" I screeched.

"You don't want them? I thought that's why you went over there—I didn't mean to spoil the invitation." Then he added, laughing, "I thought she was your BFF," proud that he managed to use a thing we had just heard on television in a sentence.

"No, I do not care to have them here for our family dinner."

"You girls have a spat?"

"Don't be silly."

"Well, too late now. They're coming. Joseph even offered to bring the cake."

"June-bug does that."

"She's got a mighty full plate. I called her and told her not to bother."

The show came back on. I didn't hear a single word. When we went to bed, I couldn't fall asleep for hours; then, when I did, I dreamed of demons, Echo the way she looked beside the fire, her eyebrows all pitched. Slithering snakes. I woke and slept, woke and slept, until I no longer knew whether I was asleep or waking. Bible verses swam in my head. Cackling laughter. Deuteronomy 22:22: *If a man is found lying with the wife of another man, both of them shall die, the man who lay with the woman, and the woman.* Matthew 12:43: *When the unclean spirit has gone out of a person, it passes through waterless places seeking rest, but finds none. Then it says, 'I will return to my house from which I came.' And when it comes, it finds the house empty, swept, and put in order. Then it goes and brings with it seven other spirits more evil than itself, and they enter and dwell there, and the last state of that person is worse than the first. So also will it be with this generation.* Ephesians 5:5: *For you may be sure of this, that everyone who is sexually immoral or impure, or who is covetous (that is, an idolater), has no inheritance in the kingdom of Christ and God.*

I woke up more tired than when I had gone to bed. If not for the fact that I missed the Sunday after the roast, I would have skipped church. I sat, numb in the pew, didn't hear a thing the preacher said. I asked Oakley if he minded if we skipped the social hour and went home, said I couldn't shake my headache. If he hadn't stopped to talk Rich Samuels, I would have been in the car before Sally Jacobs caught me outside the door, at the bottom of the church steps.

"Not going to the social?" she asked.

"A bit of a headache," I said.

"Wonderful pig roast," she said.

"Thank you." I was glad to see Rich Samuels leaving Oakley.

"I must say, you are good at keeping a secret—not telling us about that Echo woman."

"What? That she has two husbands? The polygamy?"

I hadn't intended to say it. I didn't even realize the words were coming out of my mouth until they was said—maybe it was the word *secret* that triggered my response—though maybe I did mean to say it, because I didn't feel sorry.

"What?" Sally grabbed my upper arm. "I was talking about her being Jewish."

"I didn't know myself, the polygamy," said I. "Not until the roast. I'm still processing it."

Romans 12:19: *Vengeance is mine, I will repay saith the Lord.*

My stomach roiled. I felt about to vomit right on Sally's purple-flowered blouse.

"Look, I think I'm going to be sick. I've gotta go." Oakley come up to me right at that moment. We left Sally standing there, her jaw hanging open like a country-road mailbox.

I don't like to think about when Joseph, Harry, Echo, and the girls showed up that night with the big cake with peach icing and orange script that read in swirly letters: Mark 12:31: *Thou shalt love thy neighbor as thyself.*

"You should have seen us last night," said Echo. "Sitting around Googling Bible verses. We wanted to get just the right one for you."

"When you don't know the Bible well, it's hard—you might get one out of context. I don't remember much from Hebrew school," said Joseph. "We didn't want to make fools of ourselves"—he looked at Oakley—"your wife is a regular Bible scholar, you know."

Oakley beamed. Now, just conjuring that moment in my mind, I wince.

I don't like to think about the month that followed either. All the things folks said, like that Joseph's stutter come from being forced to watch his wife and Harry have sex. That the little girls were involved. Child services was out there two or three times. Pickup trucks squealed by the house in the dead of night, teenage boys shouting obscenities. Mud and firecrackers in their mailbox. A body spray-painted "whore house" in big, black, spidery letters on the side of the orange barn that faced the road. A gang of teens slung cow manure that plastered the front porch.

"Just kids," said Oakley. But I noticed he didn't go offer to help clean up like he would have with any other neighbor. He didn't forbid me when I went to help, but he clearly didn't approve. "How could you have known such a thing and not told me? We have to live here."

Fortunately, the girls had each other at school. And the county had come into the twenty-first century, so the no-bullying rule was enforced. Not like when I was young and the chicken farmers' kids got tortured from time to time or Sally got made fun of. But no one spoke to the twins. A playdate or joining the 4-H was out of the question. In mid-October, the family moved back to New York.

The day the moving van came, Echo walked across the road to sit on my porch.

"Someone must have seen Harry and me kissing in the parking lot outside Mike's Market," said Echo. When the movers started carrying out furniture, she said, "I can't watch this. Let's take a walk."

As we started up the road, she took my hand. I tingled. My heart swelled. I felt like a schoolgirl again, before Amy had dropped me.

"It was the Monday after your party. It's the only thing I can think of. I know I should have been more discreet, but I had missed him so much."

I could only nod.

"I hope it's not going to be hard for you. Just keep telling them you didn't know," said Echo, dropping my hand. "A car could come flying over the ridge. I wouldn't want anyone to see us holding hands—who knows what they would say."

I still didn't say anything. If there was ever a time to fess up, it was that moment. But the inside of my head had gone crazy again with Bible verses, round and round, over and over, particularly Matthew 24:10: *And then shall many be offended, and shall betray one another, and shall hate one another.*

"You do have to visit me in New York," said Echo. I know she meant it when she spoke, but I also knew that once she was back in the city she would want nothing more than to forget about her time in the central farmlands of

Michigan. She would push me from her head. I only wished I could push her so easily from mine.

The following year, I received the envelope from Harry in the mail. Inside was a cutting from newspaper article with a large photo of his installation, an orange barn about the size of a washer or dryer, scribbled with Biblical quotations, roped off in the middle of a museum space. Out the front door of the little barn poured hundreds of dirty peach pits, like a gaping mouth spitting out ugly words. I stared at the photo for a long time, then put it at the bottom of my sewing box. I pull it out now and again, trying to figure out what it means, wondering if he was trying to tell me he knows what I did.

Of course, all that really matters is that I know.

Acknowledgments

Thank you to the following journals, where the below stories were originally published, some in slightly different form:

"Hors d'oeuvres," *StoryQuarterly*; "Slow Dance," *december magazine* (where it received Honorable Mention in the 2022 Curt Johnson Prose Awards); "Ogden, Ohio," (originally called "The Moment in the Middle"), *Connecticut Review*; "Noir," *Solstice Literary Magazine* (Editors' Pick); "Her Life in Parties," *Fifth Wednesday*; "Wheels," *Hypertext Magazine*; "Maternal Instinct," *Fiction Southeast*; "JUMP," *Bright Flash Literary Review*; and "The Goodbye Party," *Cimarron Review*.

Gratitude to the wonderful people who helped bring this book to fruition: My amazing writing group, the Persisters, which includes Rosellen Brown, Janet Burroway, Tsivia Cohen, Maggie Kast, Peggy Shinner, Sharon Solwitz, and S. L. Wisenberg; Victoria Anderson, who read the manuscript from start to finish and gave insightful suggestions; Elizabeth Shepherd, who read many components along the way and provided sage advice; my writing and reading friends who provided support and inspiration, some from the time I started writing: Sara Livingston, Sharon Evans, Grant McCorkill, Cathy Mellett, Susan Sink, Jeanne Petrolle, Sarah Pressman Lovinger, Kim Green, Cilla Murray, Joann Connington, Jody Becker, Tom Bachtell, Molly Taylor, Marni Rebmann; my family, who even when not reading my work, are always inspiring (Jim, Rory, Susie, Wendy, Will, Vivian, Bret, Tommy, aka Rozy, Pete, & Lynn, Kaitlin, and Jamie in Portland); the kind folks at the University of Wisconsin Press, particularly Dennis Lloyd and Jacqueline Krass: my great teachers, particularly Stuart Dybek who has been reading my work for many years; all the people I am momentarily forgetting; and my amazing (and patient) husband, Fred.

About the Author

Cravings is Garnett Kilberg Cohen's fourth collection of short stories. The first three include *Lost Women, Banished Souls* (University of Missouri Press), *How We Move the Air* (Mayapple Press), and *Swarm to Glory* (Wiseblood Books). She has also published nonfiction and poetry, including a chapbook called *Passion Tour* (Finishing Line Press). Her essays have appeared in *The Rumpus, Witness, The Antioch Review,* and *The New Yorker* online, among others. Her awards include an Illinois Artist's Fellowship for Prose, the Crazyhorse Fiction Prize, and two Notable Essay citations from *Best American Essays.*

A professor at Columbia College Chicago for over thirty years, Garnett has served in various editorial positions at *Another Chicago Magazine, South Loop Review, Punctuate: A Nonfiction Magazine,* and *Fifth Wednesday.* She earned her BA magna cum laude from the University of Cincinnati and her MFA in creative writing from the University of Pittsburgh.